"Are you threatening me?" he asked incredulously

He felt another bubble of laughter start deep in his chest, but he figured it might be best to suppress it, even if this situation reminded him of a mouse going after a lion.

"What would you lose by giving me a chance?"

The respect of every man in the business, he thought wryly. A woman on Blaze Hamilton's crew? Not if hell froze over....

Quinn Wilder is a journalism graduate who claims her training took something she loved and turned it into an "ordinary old job." In writing fiction, she rediscovered her passion for transforming blank stationery into a magical world she can disappear into for days at a time. Quinn likes camping, swimming in cold lakes on sizzling summer days, riding horses over open meadows and swooping down mountains on skis. She makes her home in British Columbia's Okanagan Valley and finds it a peaceful setting in which to weave tales, as well as being a wonderful playground for her and her family.

Books by Quinn Wilder

HARLEQUIN ROMANCE

Don't miss any of our special offers. Write to us at the following address for information on our newest releases.

Harlequin Reader Service
U.S.: 3010 Walden Ave., P.O. Box 1325, Buffalo, NY 14269
Canadian: P.O. Box 609, Fort Erie, Ont. L2A 5X3

BUILD A DREAM
Quinn Wilder

Harlequin Books

TORONTO • NEW YORK • LONDON
AMSTERDAM • PARIS • SYDNEY • HAMBURG
STOCKHOLM • ATHENS • TOKYO • MILAN
MADRID • WARSAW • BUDAPEST • AUCKLAND

If you purchased this book without a cover you should be aware that this book is stolen property. It was reported as "unsold and destroyed" to the publisher, and neither the author nor the publisher has received any payment for this "stripped book."

For my man,
Rob,
with gratitude and wonder
for the dreams
we build together
one day at a time

ISBN 0-373-17238-9

BUILD A DREAM

Copyright © 1993 by Quinn Wilder.

First North American Publication 1995.

All rights reserved. Except for use in any review, the reproduction or utilization of this work in whole or in part in any form by any electronic, mechanical or other means, now known or hereafter invented, including xerography, photocopying and recording, or in any information storage or retrieval system, is forbidden without the written permission of the publisher, Harlequin Enterprises Limited, 225 Duncan Mill Road, Don Mills, Ontario, Canada M3B 3K9.

All characters in this book have no existence outside the imagination of the author and have no relation whatsoever to anyone bearing the same name or names. They are not even distantly inspired by any individual known or unknown to the author, and all incidents are pure invention.

This edition published by arrangement with Harlequin Enterprises B.V.

® and TM are trademarks of the publisher. Trademarks indicated with ® are registered in the United States Patent and Trademark Office, the Canadian Trade Marks Office and in other countries.

Printed in U.S.A.

CHAPTER ONE

'AND I don't give a damn if you were held up by a herd of stampeding elephants crossing the street...'

Janey slid out of her little red Volkswagen Beetle convertible, unnoticed. She shut the door quietly, thrust her sunglasses over her hazel eyes, yanked a blue baseball cap over her shining cap of light brown curls, and crossed her arms over her chest. She walked around to the other side of her car, leaned her behind against the round mudguard over her right front tyre, and watched.

'And you expect me to eat seventy bucks an hour, and just have that truck sitting there spinning concrete, while you're...'

His language turned quite colourful and a little smile tickled Janey's lips. She supposed you didn't get christened with a nickname like Blaze for being mild-mannered.

He was a big man, and shirtless. Faded, filthy jeans rode low on his flat hips and moulded the hard contours of his legs and buttocks.

'That's the third time, and that's more chances than I usually give...'

This was followed by another rather astonishing stream of expletives. He was gesticulating as he spoke, and the bulging muscles in his arms rippled every time he moved.

Janey noticed the other man back away from him half a step. He was a smaller man, and it was easy to sym-

5

pathise with him. But it was a mistake to back down from a man like Blaze Hamilton.

Blaze Hamilton was tanned, and even in the mellow September sunshine a fine sheen of sweat glowed on the ridges of a chest made deep and strong by years of hard, physical work with hammer and nails and concrete and wood.

'No way! If you'd been on bloody time...'

His eyes, azure as a summer sky, were snapping electric-blue sparks, and at any movement, she suspected, he was probably going to throw the hammer that he held in one big, scarred hand.

'You're wasting my time. You're out of here.' He snapped a thumb towards the road and abruptly he spun around to his job site, his broad, heavily muscled back turned, dismissing the employee who had made the mistake of being late for a concrete pour.

The fired man passed her, his head down. He glanced up at her as he passed, his black eyes full of anger and humiliation.

She felt sorry for him, and looked back at Blaze Hamilton. She felt a raw wave of anger.

Another life casually destroyed by him.

Her eyes followed the line of that back as his hands moved to rest on his hips for a moment. The unblemished surface went from being impossibly broad at his shoulders to extremely narrow where it slipped out of view into the band of his blue jeans.

She felt he'd been far harsher than the circumstances seemed to warrant, but then she had known that was what she was dealing with. A harsh man.

Besides, his firing someone just as she arrived was a coincidence working in her favour. She tried not to think if that dismissed worker had a wife he had to break the news to, children he had to feed . . .

He moved his hand off his hip and pushed it through hair thick and blond and sun-streaked to nearly white in places. He stood still for maybe thirty seconds, surveying the scene.

Powerful and impatient, she thought, a dangerous combination. Well, she already knew that, too—that he was a dangerous man.

She had been sixteen the last time she had seen him. Eight years had passed. His face was more weathered, but other than that he was unchanged. It didn't seem fair. Her whole world had changed that night, or started to change. The seeds of destruction that he had planted had come to their full fruition only two weeks ago.

She bit hard on her lip. She couldn't think of that now. She had to be strong, not weak. She had to be at least as strong as he was if she was ever going to see justice done. It was an intimidating thought.

As she watched him, she could see a knot of tension dissolve from his shoulders, as if he found comfort in the scene he was surveying. Two other men were at work. One of them was a monster of a man, at least six feet six, built like a tank, and shaggy as a sheepdog. The other man was older, small and wiry, yet strong. There was something closed and cold in his face.

Rough and tough men, all three of them. And yet she felt a certain comfort in surveying this scene, too. Not everybody would understand that. And certainly not Jonathan. In a few days the skeleton of a house would stand here, but at the moment she was looking at a hole in the ground with fresh footings poured.

Blaze Hamilton was a building contractor for residential construction. Some said he was the best in this business, though her loyalty lay in another direction.

Her dad had done the best work in the business. She'd grown up on his job sites, playing in the sand beneath the unfinished houses when she was very young, later, learning, almost through osmosis, how to read a plan, and lay concrete, frame a house, put in the floors, and the walls and the windows and the roof.

Her father had always said proudly she was a born builder, and she was. It was on these rugged construction sites that she felt contentment. It was with sweat in her eyes and her muscles straining that she felt happiness.

She had tried hard to find a more feminine pursuit that made her as happy. She had a degree in education and had tried teaching. She had hated it. Not the children, but being inside, being imprisoned inside a room when the sun was shining or the rain was slashing down in ecstatic torrents. She couldn't stand the stillness of the classroom. She liked moving, she liked a day that held a few more physical challenges than 'and then we all fall down'.

Then she had tried working in a library and hated that, too, for all the same reasons that she had hated teaching and one more...the quiet. She liked noise—the thumping of hammers and the whine of Skilsaws, the voices of men.

Next, she had worked in a dentist's office. She had hated that job the worst of all. It was too quiet, too inactive, too indoors...and, worst of all, she had met a computer that hated her guts. On the plus side, though, she had also met Jonathan...

She frowned at the thought of her fiancé. He was not going to be thrilled that she had come here today, even though he'd been appalled by her quickly deteriorating relationship with the office computer.

She squared her shoulders. Two weeks ago, this decision had been made for her. She was here to revenge her family's honour. If she could, she was going to lay waste to Blaze Hamilton's career, just the way he'd laid waste to her father's.

She just hadn't expected to feel such a strong sense of... homecoming—as if she could be happy doing this kind of work in a way she'd never been happy in a dentist's office. Maybe when she was finished with Blaze Hamilton she'd stay in construction.

Jonathan would have a fit, but wasn't that what loving someone was about? Wanting *them* to be happy? He didn't think it would be appropriate for a dentist to have a construction worker for a wife. But he just didn't know the reality. She wouldn't wear a carpenter's apron to his high-class functions with clients. She'd only swear, and even then not very often, on the site.

He would see it would be just fine. She'd be the same person he had fallen in love with—with one big difference. She'd be contented, walking in her father's footsteps, continuing the family tradition of building that Blaze Hamilton had so cruelly and carelessly interrupted.

And she could be happy at this kind of work, if not on this particular job. Here, she must never forget her motive. Working on this house that sat high on a hill and overlooked the sweeping Okanagan Valley of British Columbia's interior, she must remember what she was really doing. Watching him. Making note of the shortcuts he took, any bribes he paid, any irregularities that went into his building.

Standing here, the smells in her nostrils, of sun on dirt and oil on concrete forms, she felt again that seducing sensation of homecoming. Strange to feel that on the building site of the man who had destroyed her home and her family... and her father.

She'd get him, if it was the last thing she ever did. Maybe.

There was one very large obstacle to overcome. And he was stalking towards her now, impatience clear in the faint downturn of those straight lips, and in the narrowness of blue eyes.

'I think that kid must be waiting to see you, Blaze.'

'Huh?' Blaze turned and looked down at the road. 'Aw, hell!'

He'd told the employment office to send him an experienced carpenter's helper. He'd known for a week Raoul had to go. It was no good having a drinker on a job. Still, he'd hoped the employment office could give him something before things came to a head with Raoul.

They'd given him 'something' all right. Some kid in a baseball cap who'd probably just quit high school. The boy looked incredibly young behind those sunglasses, and like a weakling besides. There wasn't enough muscle in those arms to lift a box of staples.

Today, he decided sourly, was not his day. He was glad it was just about over. He could go home. He thought of Melanie, and sighed. She probably had tickets to something or other. And then she'd be mad when he either fell asleep or squirmed during the performance.

Melanie was easily the most beautiful woman he had ever seen. She was tall and as blonde as he was. Sun-kissed and golden. Only he knew now that the blonde came from a bottle and the gold came from a tanning salon. He sighed. He seemed to attract the same type over and over again. Spoiled, helpless women whose sole ambition in life seemed to be to make him over into something he was not.

He was a building contractor. A carpenter. That was what he liked being. He liked getting his hands dirty, and watching houses, *his* houses, emerge from where there was nothing before. He didn't want to be sophisticated, or high-powered. He had no interest in being an entrepreneur or an investor.

Impatiently, he leaped over troughs surrounding his house site, and went down to the road.

'What can I do for you?' His voice was deliberately cold. On a closer look, the boy was fine-featured and girlish. A construction crew would eat him for breakfast.

The sunglasses came up, and Blaze was astounded to find himself staring into eyes green and gold and dancing with a certain defiance. At least now he knew why the boy looked like a girl. The boy *was* a girl.

'The employment office said you had a job open.'

That caught him off balance. 'If your boyfriend wants a job, he'll have to apply himself.'

Interesting pink highlights crept into those high cheekbones. She wasn't a beautiful woman, he thought, but there was certainly something about her that was attractive. Some depth in the sparkling green-gold of those eyes.

He reminded himself, sternly, that he had enough women problems. Besides which, this one was not his type. She was too small and lithe. Undeniably feminine, but built like the boy he'd mistaken her for.

'*I'm* applying for the job.'

There was a hint of steel in that husky voice that took him by surprise. Still, it didn't keep him from laughing.

'You? You must be joking!' He laughed again 'You seem to be a little confused about the meaning of the term "homemaker".'

The baseball cap was whipped off and held in a clenched fist. His eyes strayed to the sun-kissed brown curls of her hair . She was like a little nymph, he thought, with amusement, like a little woodland nymph. An *angry* little woodland nymph.

'I am entirely serious,' she said, her voice controlled despite the anger that shot her eyes with furious sparks of gold.

He crossed his arms over his naked chest and stood looking down at her. Way down. If she was five feet three, he'd be surprised.

'I wouldn't hire a woman for this kind of work. It's too rough.'

'That's the kind of statement that can land you right in front of the Human Rights Commission, Mr Hamilton.'

'Are you threatening me?' he asked incredulously. He felt another bubble of laughter start deep in his chest, but he figured it might be best to suppress it, even if this situation reminded him of a mouse going after a lion.

'All I'm asking is for a chance. What would you lose by giving me a chance?'

The respect of every man in the business, he thought wryly. A woman on Blaze Hamilton's crew? Not if hell froze over.

'The answer is no.'

Those eyes narrowed at him, and he was reminded of a kitten about to show some frustrated claw.

'You're not going to find anyone else.'

He shrugged. He knew that was probably true. The building industry was hot this year. Every man capable of lifting a hammer seemed to be working right now. Still, he'd work a little harder himself before he hired a woman.

'If you don't hire me I'm filing a complaint with the Human Rights Commission.'

She said that quietly, leaving him not a doubt that she meant it.

'It's still a free world, sister. This is my business and I'll hire who I want.'

'It's against the law to discriminate,' she told him, her voice snapping with indignation.

'I'm not discriminating, I'm exercising free choice.' He wondered why his mood seemed to be improving from sparring with this little vixen. He noticed she had very definite curves under the cut of a man's blue denim shirt. He studied her frankly. He might as well be branded a sexist as well as a chauvinist.

He grinned at her expression, her outrage being evident in the spreading pink spots in her cheeks.

'You don't really want to come to work for a big bad wolf like me, do you?' he asked, making his voice obnoxious and sultry.

'I could handle you, and ten more just like you,' she said without batting an eye.

His ego felt the full impact of that one, and he glared at her. 'You're a pretty cocky little thing, aren't you?'

'I've got three brothers. I grew up on sites like this one. I'm good at what I do. I don't shock easily, and I can handle anything you throw at me.'

'Sure,' he said drily.

He had a picture of himself sitting on the phone again tonight, dialling numbers and hearing the same thing over and over.

Nope.

I'm working.

I'm busy.

Maybe in a few months.

I've started my own contracting company.

Sorry, Blaze.

And Melanie sitting across the room, her full red-painted lips pulled into a pout that he supposed she thought was sexy.

This woman in front of him didn't have a speck of paint on her face. She looked fresh and real. In other circumstances he wondered if he might want to get to know her. Probably not. She was probably the type he passed right by.

'Sorry, I'm not hiring.'

Something flashed in her face, just for a moment. Not anger and not a threat. Something crestfallen, like a small child who had screwed up all her nerve to ask for a special favour, only to be told no.

He felt something in him soften. Dammit, that should be warning enough not to have a woman on the job. His sympathy didn't last a full minute—because her voice was hard when she spoke. 'I'm going to file a complaint right now. See you in court.'

He had a tremendous urge to let loose on her the way he'd just let loose on Raoul. But that had been a mistake.

He already knew that. He should at least have tried to keep him on until he had someone to replace him.

So he bit back his urge to tell her to go take a flying leap, and considered the inconvenience of being dragged through court. Could they force him to hire her against his will? Probably, he realised. Equal rights were a front-page issue right now. It wouldn't do his company any good to get that kind of attention.

Besides, it would be easier—and more fun—to see how long she could last if he gave her his best shot at getting rid of her. He bet he could drive her into the ground inside of an hour. Half a day at most. That would show her to threaten Blaze Hamilton. Little chit.

He shrugged, deliberately hooding his eyes. 'OK. You win. See you tomorrow.'

Her face brightened. It made her look pretty in an earthy, elfin sort of way. It made him aware he had just made a big mistake. He probably should have gone to court. She'd probably been bluffing, anyway.

'Of course, you probably won't last a day.' Especially a day like tomorrow, he thought, when they would be setting up concrete forms to pour the foundation walls. It was hard, filthy work and his crew would probably lose no time in initiating her.

They gave rookies a hard time. Male rookies. That was traditional. They'd eat *her* alive. Maybe that was a lesson she needed to learn. Women didn't belong in male professions. Especially not tiny little women who looked about as tough as the petals on a buttercup.

'I want twelve dollars an hour to start,' she said firmly.

He stared at her in surprise. Give an inch, he thought wryly. 'I'll give you ten. If you're worth more, you'll get it. I always pay people what they're worth.' He wondered what her cheque would be for. Thirty dollars, he bet himself with satisfaction.

'In that case, in two weeks,' she said with husky confidence, 'I'll be the highest paid member of your crew.'

'Yeah, sure. I start at seven. If you're late, don't bother coming.'

'I won't be late.'

He looked at that small earnest face and sighed. No, she probably wouldn't be, dammit.

He swung abruptly away from her. Something had just happened that he hadn't wanted to happen. And if there was something he was rather famous for it was being in complete control of every situation.

'Hey, Moose,' he roared, 'what the hell are you doing? I don't pay you to sit around and study your fingernails...'

He slid a look back over his shoulder to see if she looked intimidated. If he yelled at her like that she'd probably start bawling. Geez. He didn't know if he could bear it—even for three hours.

She was behind the wheel of her Volkswagen. She did a neat U-turn, gave him a jaunty and very unintimidated wave and roared off.

'Hey, who was the chick, boss?'

Chick. He smiled grimly to himself. She was the type of woman who wouldn't much like being called a chick. His smile deepened. One hour. Maybe two.

He favoured Moose with a rare smile. Moose was a fixture on his crew for a reason that neither of them fully understood. He was big and lazy and had to be ridden every minute to get an honest day's work out of him. He was also about as foul-mouthed and obnoxious as they came—even in this business.

He could count on Moose to be rough and vulgar enough to turn off that little snip, and send her running back to the safety of the bank teller's window or waiting on tables, where she belonged.

He realised he didn't even know her name. And he'd need it for her separation slip when she quit.

If he'd planned it, it couldn't have been better, he thought, surveying the building site by the early morning light with fiendish satisfaction.

It was pouring with rain. He'd seen pigpens that looked a lot less muddy than the building site looked right now. Some moron from the form company had dropped the forms—the long wooden pieces that would hold the concrete in place until it hardened into walls—off on the pavement instead of bringing them up to the house site. They were going to have to be hauled, by hand, uphill over about fifty yards of mud of the finest quality. The kind that acted as though it had been mixed with cement, that clung in great hunks to boots and made them seem to weigh about fifty pounds each.

He knew just the person who was going to do the hauling, too. Ha. If she even showed up. Probably scared of the rain. Probably wouldn't want to get her hair wet. Probably didn't like mud and dirt. Women, as a rule, didn't.

Her little red Volkswagen careened around the corner.

'Aw, hell,' he muttered to himself. Well, the lady was about to find out that bull work was not meant for cute little fillies. A smile flickered across his wet face.

He glanced at his watch. Five to seven. Let the games begin, he said to himself. He started whistling.

Janey got out of her car. She didn't like the look of that smile. He was standing, arms folded over that great chest, watching her. He seemed impervious to the rain that slid off his yellow oilskin coat. He wasn't even wearing the hood, and the water was running in rivulets off his fair hair.

She shrugged into an oilskin coat that was almost identical to his. She turned and surveyed the site. It was a mess. Still, she'd never minded the rain. It had always felt better to her to be out in it than sitting inside feeling like its prisoner, somehow. And she knew what concrete work was like. It was a mess even without the complication of rain, and she'd dressed for it. Her jeans were nearly falling apart, they were so old. The knee was out of one leg and a pocket missing from the back.

She walked up to him, trying for dignity, which was very hard with the mud sucking at her boots. She noted his eyes narrow on her with a touch of surprise. He hadn't even expected her to know how to dress. She hoped she was going to surprise him a lot today—and in the days that followed.

'Good morning,' she said brightly.

'Not great,' he answered back. 'You can start putting those forms in the hole.'

Janey looked at him steadily. They both knew this would be her weakness. She didn't have the physical strength of a man. There were lots of jobs she could do as well as any man, but this was not one of them.

She shrugged, pulled some leather gloves from her pocket and shoved her hands into them.

He snorted.

Her eyes moved to his hands. They were big and muscled, scarred and callused. No, she wanted to get even, but she had to protect her hands. Jonathan had been less than thrilled last night when she had told him about the job. Downright disapproving, in fact. There was no need to fuel his ire by ending up with beaten-up hands. She had almost wished, last night, she could tell him the whole story, but she couldn't. Not yet. He might try to stop her.

'I think you're just reacting to the stress of your dad being hospitalised,' Jonathan had said.

That was close enough to the truth.

She went to the stack of forms and eyed them. The wiry man she had noticed yesterday skidded down the muddy hill and hefted two of them on to his narrow shoulders.

'Hi,' she said, 'I'm Janey.'

Cold blue eyes sized her up. He didn't nod and he didn't offer his own name. He didn't even look surprised. Just indifferent. He went on with his work.

Well, she hadn't exactly expected high tea at the Empress, and she wasn't here to make friends. In fact that would only complicate what she was here to do.

She might as well get the eight-footers out of the way, while her energy was high. She slid one off the stack, and heaved it up on to her shoulder. It was impossibly heavy, but, setting her lips in a determined line, she slipped and slid her way up the rise.

It was going to be a long morning.

'Moose, it's five after seven. What are you? A banker?'

She didn't pause, but caught the arrival of her co-worker out of the corner of her eye. He was the big one. He had shaggy mud-coloured hair that fell over mud-coloured eyes. He looked like a gorilla, partly because his shoulders were badly stooped. She wondered if he was shy, if his size had made him self-conscious when he was younger and he had developed that habit of hunching. She smiled at him.

His mouth dropped open. 'Boss, that's a dame.'

'Yeah. No kidding.'

'Well, how come?'

'I guess nobody told her women belong in the kitchen. She'll figure it out, though.'

He's trying to make me mad, Janey thought. He's trying to make me lose it, so he can legitimately fire me—if he couldn't pound her into the mud first. It was going to be a *very* long morning. She could feel those blue eyes resting on her, waiting for some reaction. She kept her face carefully blank.

'Let's get these forms up there,' he growled.

Janey could lift one. Moose came and grabbed four off the pile, hefted them on to his shoulder and charged up the hill with them. She cursed softly under her breath, then whirled when there was a gravelly chuckle nearly in her ear.

'You're going to take twice as long to do half the work. You don't belong here.'

She found her eyes caught in the challenging electric-blue current of his. For some reason—she hoped it was anger—she could feel a pink stain crawling up her cheeks.

'I want a fair chance to show you what I can do.'

'You're going to get it,' he snapped, 'but don't blame me when you don't like it very much.'

'I like this fine,' she said tautly. 'You were the one complaining—already.'

'Well, can I help it? I already found something to complain about. Geeze, you barely have enough muscle in those arms to lift a teacup.'

'I happen to be very strong, for a woman. Obviously my value isn't going to be in hefting forms. But I can do it, and I won't complain about it.'

He swore under his breath. 'I've had a woman on the site ten minutes, and we're already wasting time wagging our tongues.'

'You're the one who started it!' she sputtered indignantly, grabbing a form and putting it on her shoulder. 'Now get out of my way.'

She noticed with some satisfaction that his mouth fell open, then snapped shut. He wasn't used to people telling *him* to move! But a man like that had to be shown right away you weren't intimidated by him. And he had to be shown that even if you were! It was probably going to be the most satisfying experience of her life bringing him to his knees!

She pushed past him and then Moose, who gave her a sidelong look that was something between reverence and wariness.

Blaze glared at Moose. He was supposed to be giving her a hard time. Instead he was looking a bit like a frightened schoolboy who didn't know how to behave at the headmistress's garden party.

'Gee, boss, she's just a wee thing. It ain't right to be making her pack stuff.'

They both looked after her. She was already soaked, mud-slicked clean through to her skin. It was a deeply perturbing sight seeing how those wet jeans clung to her curves. There was going to be no forgetting she was a woman. The look Blaze gave Moose was several shades blacker than the weather. He stormed up the hill and passed her sliding back down.

'Leave the eight-footers for Moose,' he said, feeling as if he was making a huge concession. 'You can get the four-footers up there.'

'I'll do the eight,' she said stubbornly. She didn't need any favours from Blaze Hamilton!

'You'll do as you're told or you'll get the hell off my job.' Now what am I doing? he asked himself wearily. The whole idea was to get her off the job—and the eight-footers would have done that a whole hell of a lot quicker than the four.

They stood there glaring at each other for a few seconds. She looked like a half-drowned rat. She tossed her head proudly, scattering raindrops, and moved away from him.

He stared after her angrily. He'd just done her a favour, for Pete's sake. Something told him having a woman on this job was about to turn into the worst experience of his life.

He glared at his watch. Twenty minutes and he suspected she was not even close to quitting. Not even close. If the set of that pointed little jaw was any indication, *he* was more likely to quit than her.

He should have taken his chances in court.

CHAPTER TWO

JANEY was covered in mud. Every bone in her body ached, and every muscle complained. Her hair was slicked to her head like an otter's. She sat on top of a pile of studs, took a bite of her sandwich and closed her eyes. The sun had come out and she lifted her face to it.

She felt good. To have made it. There were times this morning when she had thought she could not go on. But she had conjured up a picture of her father, sitting in that wheelchair, complete desolation in the sag of his head and shoulders, and a new spurt of energy would go through her.

Eight years ago, he had been a vital man, unbelievably strong. The doctors said his current state of health was because he'd abused tobacco for too many years, that his heart just couldn't handle it. But she knew differently. His heart had been just fine until that night eight years ago. He'd had his first heart attack only days after that visit from Blaze.

Moose, and Tuffy, as she heard Blaze calling the other men, were sitting on a different stack of lumber. Neither had made any effort to talk to her, but then she noticed that they weren't talking to each other, either. Moose seemed curious about her, but the other man continued to seem resolutely indifferent.

Telling herself she didn't care, she lay down on the stack of lumber and closed her eyes, hoping lunch-hour would never end.

He'd thought she'd have had it by now. He'd thought she would have given up. Thrown in the towel and gone home.

Instead she'd worked steadily all morning. It was true she didn't accomplish as much as any self-respecting man over a hundred pounds could have done. Well, that wasn't quite true. She'd done more work this morning than Raoul had done in the entire two weeks that he'd been on staff. Raoul, who had somehow perfected the art of looking as if he was working, but managed to accomplish nothing. Or who 'disappeared' for long periods of time, and always came back just about the time Blaze noticed he was missing, looking slightly glazed and smelling, overwhelmingly, of aftershave and chewing gum.

OK, so she was a better bargain than Raoul. That was a big deal! OK, he'd been surprised by how much she did do, working away steadily, with that determined, calm look on her face. That still didn't mean she had any right to be here. He should have stuck with the eight-foot forms. Then she wouldn't have the audacity to be lying there looking strangely contented. That was the puzzle, all right. He'd worked her into the ground, or tried to, and there she lay, looking as supple and relaxed as a cat in the sun—looking ready for whatever he threw at her next. Which was going to be something good!

He stared at the expression on Moose's face, and cursed under his breath. That look was precisely why women didn't belong on jobs like this. Moose didn't do a decent day's work, anyway, and now the poor fellow had been tossed completely out of his comfort zone by the appearance of this young woman on sacred male territory.

Pretty weak reason to be trying to fire someone, Blaze, a little voice inside his head chided him. Is that the best you could do for the whole morning?

'Aw, shut up,' he said out loud.

His employees' heads swung towards him.

'Get to work,' he snapped. 'What do you think this is? A garden party at Buckingham Palace?'

He stole a covert look at his watch. He was cutting their lunchtime by ten minutes. He hoped one of them would have the nerve to complain. And he hoped it would be her!

He watched her pack up her lunch things, and stand and stretch, pressing her feminine little curves against that man's shirt that made her look more feminine than ever.

He had to get rid of her. That was all there was to it.

'Hey, runt, get my level out of my truck, on the double, and when you've done that...'

'Ohh.' Janey sank into the hot water of her bath-tub gratefully. She nearly cried when her blistered hands hit the water. It was nearly an hour later when the ringing of the phone probably saved her from drowning.

She scrambled, soaking wet, for the telephone.

'Darling, it's Jonathan. I'll come around eight to get you for the movie, all right?'

She wanted to say yes. She had to say yes. But she couldn't. She was so exhausted she couldn't even contemplate getting dressed. About the only thing she was capable of doing was walking the four or five steps it was to her bedroom and collapsing on to the bed.

'I can't, Jonathan, not tonight.'

Even the silence seemed disapproving.

'Why not?'

Temptations ran through her mind. Her long-lost sister had arrived unexpectedly from Bella Bella? No, Jonathan knew she didn't have a sister. Her grandmother had died? No, everyone used that one. Besides, she loved her grandmother. She, Janey, had come down with a strange disease. The purple, strawberry-shaped spots breaking out all over her body looked highly contagious.

Why am I thinking of lying to the man I want to marry? she asked herself, horrified to be discovering such a large defect of character in herself at such a late date.

'I'm tired, Jonathan.' Let the chips fall where they may.

Again there was that long pause that she interpreted as being disapproving. 'Well, I guess there was a benefit to being a secretary after all, wasn't there? At least you weren't too tired to go to a movie at night.'

'I'm just not in shape. Give me a week or so.'

'I'm hoping you won't last a week.'

'Well, you aren't the only one,' she murmured.

'Did they give you a hard time?'

'No harder than I expected.'

'So what did you do all day?'

She wanted to moan with exhaustion. Instead she tried to tell him.

'Doesn't that sound fun?' he commented with undisguised sarcasm.

For a moment she pictured him. Jonathan was taller than her by several inches, and slim in build. He had a remarkably handsome face, and neatly cut brown hair the identical shade of his huge, lash-fringed eyes. But his good looks could be marred by a pinched look of disapproval, and she knew that was the look that would be on his face right now.

'Look, Jonathan,' she said quietly, 'looking in people's mouths all day isn't exactly my idea of fun either, but have I ever once derided you for your choice?'

'It's not the same.'

No, she thought, being out there in the pouring rain, in the mud, straining every muscle wasn't the same as being a dentist. Or working in a dentist's office. Who could ever understand that being out in the rain felt better to her? More real, somehow. More *alive*.

'Jonathan, I'm tired and I'm crabby and I'm hanging up the phone now before we start to hate each other.'

Gently she put the phone in its cradle and stumbled off to bed.

I wonder if we're starting to hate each other? Blaze thought, eyeing Melanie from under the crook of his arm. He was sprawled on the couch, a cold Coke can in one hand, and the remote control in the other, and he wasn't moving.

'Blaze, you promised.'

'I didn't promise. Look, I've had a hard day at work. There was a stupid rookie there and I did twice as much as I normally do, and I'm not going to a movie.' Now, he thought, she's going to sulk.

He slid her a look. She floated down on to a chair, and sighed. Her lip started to quiver. He pretended to watch TV.

'I really wanted to see this film. It's been nominated for the Critic's Choice Awards.'

'So, go!' he exploded. Geez, he'd watched that little pipsqueak of a thing go up and down that hill hauling heavy lumber about a hundred times today, and *she* hadn't complained once, even though she'd had a right to. He was willing to bet if the runt wanted to go to a movie she didn't have to have a man on her arm to hold her up.

Melanie got up, gave her golden mane a shake of pure disgust, and waltzed by him. A second later, the apartment door slammed.

Good, he thought. But he didn't feel good. And somehow even this seemed like that little squirt's fault. Well, if she thought she'd worked today, she was going to find out the meaning of the word work tomorrow.

They would be pouring the concrete. He could, of course, rent a concrete vibrator, which was the modern method of removing air from concrete. But why bother when he was trying to get rid of Little Miss Mary Sunshine?

He'd give her a hammer and let her pound away at the forms to settle the concrete and remove the air. Her arm would be about ready to fall off after an hour of that. Two hours and he'd be waving goodbye to her. Her arms would be so sore she probably wouldn't even be able to wave back!

He took the last swig of his Coke and crushed the can in his hand. Melanie hated it when he did that. She said it was a juvenile show of strength.

Well, men were supposed to be strong. And women weren't.

The little nymph had to learn that, he supposed. That there were things women did and things men did. Men actually *made* homes; homemakers did cute things to the inside of them. Everybody had to learn their place, and the half-pint had to learn a woman's place. He sighed. Just what the world needed. Another Melanie.

She knew a woman's place all right. And she firmly believed her place was to look beautiful, know the correct fork to use in any situation, and to dispense with money with not a thought to common sense or need. His money, preferably.

He felt a twinge of guilt at such a callous evaluation of Melanie. They'd been together for nearly eight months. He mostly liked her. He was just tired. He'd send her some flowers tomorrow and all would be forgiven.

He wondered, inexplicably, if anybody ever sent that little Melva Milquetoast flowers. He doubted it. What kind of man would give someone like her so much as a second thought?

The kind of man lying on his couch with a crushed Coke can in his hand, he realised with disgust. Unbidden, an image of her rose in his mind, covered with mud, her body lithe and small, her face like a pixie's, laughing as she slid through that mud. Laughing! He wondered if he could find some nice rock and shovel work for her to do the next day on the off-chance she survived vibrating the forms. That should finish her off.

If Jonathan had tried, Janey fumed, he couldn't have come up with a more wrong thing to do. Flowers! For God's sake, she was fighting for her life here as it was, without him having flowers delivered to the job. During a pour!

She read the card briefly.

'Sorry I wasn't more supportive of you last night.'

She looked at the delivery boy grinning at her, recognising how ludicrous this was. She glanced over her shoulder. Blaze had fire in his eyes, and concrete setting up!

She stuffed the flowers in her car, way down on the floor where they wouldn't taunt her all day. She hurried back to the job.

'Them were nice flowers,' Moose said.

She glared at him, waiting for the teasing. There was no mockery in that big, open face. She realised that was all he was going to say.

'Thank you, Moose,' she said gratefully. She picked up her hammer, and tried to drive those stupid flowers from her mind.

She looked balefully at the job in front of her and gritted her teeth as she pounded the outside of the form. The force seemed to reverberate back up her arms, and her forearms and biceps already ached with effort.

'My name ain't really Moose,' the big man said gruffly.

If it was troubling him to be pounding the forms by hand when there was technology available to remove some of the misery from this job, he did not indicate it by word or action.

'What is your name?' she said carefully. She wasn't sure if it was a faint overture of friendship, and she certainly didn't want to scare him away by being overly enthusiastic if it was.

'Clarence.' He kept slamming away with his hammer, his back to her. Her heart went out to him. She suspected he had taken some teasing about his name.

'Would you like me to call you that?' she asked quietly.

Those big shoulders shrugged, but Janey sensed he had probably introduced the subject because that was what he wanted to be called.

They worked in silence, Clarence with easy strength, Janey stopping to wipe sweat out of her eyes, and beginning to pant a bit from exertion.

'Do you have a boyfriend?' Clarence asked suddenly. 'Is that who sent them pretty flowers?'

'Yeah, do you have a boyfriend?' another voice, deeply mocking, echoed.

Blaze was working ahead of them, handling the chute that the concrete was rumbling down. He had seemed oblivious to her, totally absorbed in what he was doing, so his sudden interest took her by surprise.

His arms were corded with effort. He was not wearing a shirt, which seemed to be his habit, and his hair glinted like a bright halo in the sun.

'Hasn't anybody warned you about skin cancer?' she muttered, looking quickly away from him. The hard, muscled lines of his body had caused the strangest sensation to shimmer briefly through her.

A light winked on in those blue eyes, and Janey was aware that it was something of a tactical error to let him know his naked chest was somewhat perturbing to her. If he thought it would get her off his job site, he'd probably take off his trousers next!

She went back to her work, hammering with a passion, but aware now of those eyes lingering on her with faint laughter in their blue depths.

'You didn't tell us if you had a boyfriend,' he reminded her.

She wanted to say it was none of their business, but she had an unhappy feeling that that reaction would just destroy Clarence's fledgeling attempts at friendship—and not bother Blaze in the least. Besides, having a boyfriend might make him think she had far more enticing chests to think about than his!

Not that Jonathan had much of a chest. Not that it had ever mattered to her...before.

'Yes, I do.'

'Oh.' Clarence's monosyllabic reply was loaded with pathos.

'He's a dentist. We're going to be married in the winter. Probably in December.'

'Nice guy,' Blaze muttered.

'I beg your pardon?' she shot at him, never losing the rhythm of hitting the forms. She wasn't going to let that kind of comment pass unchallenged, but she wasn't going to give him an excuse to find fault with her work, either.

'There's only one reason anybody would get married in December.'

'And what's that?' she snapped.

'Tax break.'

The insinuation that a man would only marry her as a tax break was infuriating but it would be a mistake to let Blaze see she was seething inside. He would probably accept that as a victory of sorts.

'In that case,' she said sweetly, 'I hope the flowers are deductible, too.'

'Ha. There's only one reason a man sends a woman flowers,' Blaze said darkly.

'Oh? And what's that?'

'They've been fighting, of course. Dr Dentist doesn't like you doing this job, does he?'

It was surprising how much easier it was to vibrate concrete with a little angry energy behind every swing of that hammer. It was surprising how perceptive a seemingly insensitive man could be!

'It is none of your business how my fiancé feels about my job!'

He shrugged. 'I could care less, actually. Do you want to pick up the pace a bit? That cement is setting up.'

The cement was not setting up. She deliberately turned her back on him. 'You know, Clarence——'

'Clarence?' Blaze hooted, somehow having tuned out that part of her and Clarence's conversation.

It was Clarence's turn to straighten, and he gave Blaze a look that was vaguely menacing.

'I told her to call me that.'

'What on earth for?' Blaze asked incredulously.

'Because it's my name,' Clarence said quietly and stubbornly.

'This place is going to the dogs even faster than I could have predicted,' Blaze muttered, sending her a look shot through with anger.

'Anyway, Clarence,' Janey continued, making every attempt to pretend she was not in the least disturbed by the angry flashes that turned those eyes the most incredible shade of blue, 'I was just going to say that I have a friend I'd like you to meet.'

'A girl?' Blaze and Clarence asked in astonished unison.

'A woman,' she corrected them.

Her friend was Mabel, and Janey had known her since college. She was a wonderful woman—bright and funny and caring. But she was extremely tall for a woman, rangy, and not pretty by any stretch of the imagination. As far as Janey knew Mabel had never even been on a date.

Her friend loved children, and was succeeding where Janey had not—as a teacher, specialising in English as a second language, or ESL. And yet loneliness was a theme that ran through her life, and Mabel despaired of ever having children of her own, or a man who loved her. What would it hurt to introduce her to Clarence? Janey suspected they were two very lonely people.

'My friend's a teacher,' she said, pounding, wishing Blaze could shove off somewhere, instead of working in front of her, directing the cement chute, and shooting blazing blue daggers out of his eyes at every opportunity.

'A teacher?' Clarence said with awe. 'Aw, ain't no teacher gonna have nuthin' to do with me. I ain't an educated man.'

'There are things more important than education, Clarence. Character. Integrity.'

To her relief, Blaze had finally moved ahead. The pour was finished. Her relief was short-lived.

'Runt, get over here right now.'

Janey glared at Blaze, but obligingly shoved her hammer into her apron. She found herself practically being lifted out of the hole. He set her down firmly and stomped off. She followed him.

'What the hell are you doing?'

'Pardon?'

'Leave Moose alone.'

'What do you mean, leave him alone? The man's lonely.'

'The man's happy. You don't know the first thing about him. He drinks beer and tells dirty jokes. He has no couth. You're going to introduce him to a friend of yours? Just come to work, for God's sake, and don't start meddling in people's lives. That's not what men do.'

'I'm not a man.'

'Well, you should act like one if you want to do a man's job!'

'I just want to do *a* job. I am not interested in behaving like a man. For the most part, you are a bunch of insensitive louts, and you, Blaze Hamilton, lead the pack!'

'Me?' he roared.

'You! It isn't me that doesn't know a thing about Clarence, it's you. How long has he worked for you, anyway?'

'A long time.'

'Did you know it hurts his feelings to be called Moose?'

'Did he say that?'

'Well, not in so many words, but have you ever asked him what his real name was? What he'd like to be called?'

'Why would I ask him? I know him. Look, men just don't get hurt feelings the way the weaker sex does. What you're probably really saying is that it hurts your feelings when I call you runt and pipsqueak and squirt and...'

'It doesn't, because I could care less what a boor like you thinks of me——'

'A boor?' he spluttered.

'Oh, so you only like calling names, is that it?'

'Look, I'm the boss here——'

'Just try it.'

'Try what?'

'Calling him Clarence.'

'What for?'

'Because that's his name.'

'I just knew this would happen.'

'What?'

'You'd start bringing all this woman stuff here with you. Next we'll be dropping quarters in a jar every time we swear and putting white linen napkins in our lunch-boxes.'

'Does it threaten your masculinity to be civilised, Mr Hamilton?'

'Lady,' he said softly, 'don't start fooling with my masculinity. It's just a little more than a waif like you can handle.'

'There isn't anything about you I can't handle,' she said stubbornly, even though she knew she had just crossed a line into very dangerous territory.

He crossed the small distance between them in the flash of an eye. She couldn't have stepped back if she wanted to. She stood, frozen to her spot, as he swooped down on her.

Suddenly she was looking way, way up at a mountain of a man. His eyes were shooting angry sparks, and when she tried to look away from him, tried to get out of pouncing range, she found her chin captured in the hardness of his hand.

And then those lips, those sensual, strong lips, were coming down and claiming hers. She ordered herself to reach into her carpenter's apron, slide her hammer out of its holder, and bop him over the head. She ordered herself to do that, and her arms moved . . . but not to her apron.

They twined themselves shamelessly around the strong column of his throat, and she felt her lips respond to the fire of his with an astonishing fire of their own.

She was being sucked into a swirling vortex of pure sensation. As her lips answered the challenge of his, her whole body seemed to surge to life, to begin to tingle and vibrate with feelings that were foreign, exquisite, and thrillingly dangerous.

Far away, she heard the echoing sound of a hammer being dropped on concrete. Sanity struck like lightning and she broke away from him, and pushed. She knew she couldn't break the steel bond of his arms, so he must have taken mercy on her. He let her go. She stumbled backwards, and swiped hastily at her mouth, glaring at him.

'So you can handle my masculinity, can you?' His voice was full of sarcasm, his eyes cool now as a north sea. Apparently thunder had not replaced the beating of his heart, as it had within the walls of her own chest. Apparently there were no electrical currents pulsating up and down the rippling muscled surface of his arms, tormenting him and teasing him, as they were her.

'How dare you?' she spat.

'You said you could handle it,' he said blandly.

'That isn't what I meant!'

'What did you mean, then?'

'I meant I could handle your swearing and being bossy and overbearing——'

'That isn't all there is to my masculinity,' he said softly.

'So I see, you ... you impudent caveman! I could have you arrested for that, you know.'

'Sure. If you hadn't enjoyed it so much.'

'I did not!'

'Lady, I could take the sparkles in your eyes and sell them for diamonds.'

She had a ridiculous impulse to hide her eyes.

'Don't you ever do that again,' she warned him.

'I won't,' he said blandly. 'It was just to prove a point.'

Oh, thank you so much.

'And what point was that?'

'Women don't belong in these kind of work situations. It changes everything. Chemistry starts to happen. Poor old Moose is half in love with you and you've only been here two days.'

'He's not in love with me. He might be starting to like me. I have treated him with the respect and compassion he deserves.'

'He likes you because you're a woman. He likes the way you look in your blue jeans. As for compassion, I seriously doubt he would know the difference between a bonafide saint and an axe murderer.'

'He would so. But you, Mr Hamilton, probably would not.'

'I'd recognise a saint if I encountered one.' A mocking smile lifted one corner of that perturbingly sensual mouth. 'They probably don't kiss back.'

'If you ever did encounter a saint, you could single-handedly turn her into an axe murderer!'

'That's exactly what I've been trying to tell you,' he said with quiet triumph. 'Men and women seem to bring out the worst in each other when they work together like this.'

'How can you say such a thing? Many men and women work together without behaving in such a... base manner.'

'Well, dentists and the people who do this kind of work aren't exactly the same cut of cloth, you know.'

'Oh, I know!'

'For instance, when I look at your mouth, the last thing I think about is cleaning your teeth.'

'Then don't look at it any more. You don't have the impulse control of a three-year-old child.'

'I'm just used to getting everything I want,' he said silkily.

'Well, you don't want me, do you?' she squeaked.

'Lord, no!' he bellowed, obviously tiring of whatever game he'd been playing, that quick temper coming back to the surface. 'The exact opposite. I just want you out of here.'

'Too bad,' she said stubbornly, 'because I'm not going!'

'I could break you if I wanted to.'

'Give it your best shot,' she challenged.

But he surprised himself. He should have just worked her into the ground. But he didn't. He didn't even know why. It didn't have anything to do with that kiss, that was for sure. It had been a pretty chaste kind of kiss, in his book. Kind of like putting your lips to a mountain stream that was pure and clean and sweet somehow.

'Be sure and keep your stupid gloves on,' he muttered gruffly. 'The cement will rip the stuffing out of your hands.'

He saw the surprise register in her eyes.

'It would be just like a woman to file a worker's compensation claim for a few blisters.'

The surprise left her eyes. With a shake of her head, she went back to work. He watched her narrowly. She wasn't any greenhorn. She'd done all this before. And really, if he thought about it rationally, there wasn't a reason in the world why a woman couldn't do some of these things. In jobs that didn't require any strength he couldn't help but notice she was a hell of a lot faster and more conscientious than Moose had ever been.

She bent over to hammer the bottom of a form. All rational thought deserted him. He stared at her. A dentist's woman. What a waste.

She straightened. The sun poured through her shirt and he could see the firm outline of her body. The light glinted and danced in the tangle of her light brown curls.

He had to get her off his building site before she drove him crazy.

But at lunchtime she was still there.

Grudgingly he handed her the papers he was going to have to have filled out to make income tax and unemployment insurance deductions off her pay cheque. Which was going to be for something more than thirty dollars after all.

After a while, she handed him back the papers. Her handwriting was neat and tight and feminine. Her name was Janey. Janey Smith. Just about the most ordinary name he'd ever heard, and yet somehow it suited her.

Janey. It made him think of bright yellow buttercups and a pure mountain stream, and he wasn't sure why. It was probably part of this slow progression towards madness.

'Hey, boss, my pal Bud down at the Oasis said you were probably getting a grant for having a woman here, huh?'

'You told somebody at the Oasis she was here?'

'Sure. It ain't a secret, is it?'

'Not now,' he muttered. Still, Moose might have something there. He was sure he had read something in an employment circular about grants being available if a woman was hired for a non-traditional position.

Since she was here anyway, he could check into it. Besides, it would make it easier to take the ribbing he was in for when word got out if he could claim that a grant induced him to hire her. Hell, money was the bottom line for most of the guys in this business. If there was money available to hire a woman, there might be a lot more of them showing up on construction sites.

But not likely.

This seemed to be his cross to bear.

CHAPTER THREE

'Boss, don't make her carry any more of those joists. They're too heavy for her.'

'She wanted the job,' Blaze said coldly. Day Five. He'd woken up this morning with a song in his heart, *knowing* this was the day she'd go. He'd worked her twelve hours solid yesterday, doing the dirtiest work known to man ... or woman.

And this morning he'd started out with more of the same. The day was half over and the song had died in his heart.

Now he was crabby. Time to haul out the big guns. He was irritated with himself. He'd vowed he could get rid of her in three hours and now they were almost halfway through her fifth day. She was staggering, but dammit, she wasn't going down.

'You should be ashamed of yourself.'

Blaze nearly cut off his thumb with the Skilsaw. He picked up the board he'd been cutting and hurled it as hard as he could. He'd never thought he'd live to see the day Moose would be telling him he should be ashamed of himself. That was what a woman did! Ashamed. Mothers and grandmothers used words like that. Not six-foot-six construction workers.

Still, there *was* a kernel of shame in him. He supposed that was what made him so angry. He was acting like a ten-year-old boy about to lose a dare. But he wasn't going to let anybody see the shame—only the anger.

'Get back to work,' he said colourfully, glaring at Moose.

Moose folded his tree-trunk arms across the barrel of his chest. 'The joists are too heavy for her.'

'So? Let her tell me that if it's a problem.'

'She's too proud. She'd bust her heart proving she could carry those things.'

'So let her,' he muttered.

'You give her a different job, or I walk.'

Blaze couldn't believe his ears. He and Moose had worked together for seven years. That little chit! She'd changed Moose's loyalty with a vague promise of introducing him to a friend. Changed his loyalty by looking great in blue jeans!

Still, something in Moose's tone stopped him from blowing up. He slid a look over to where she was trying to wrestle an eighteen-foot floor joist off the pile. It was a kind of funny sight, and yet he didn't feel any laughter.

He found himself striding towards her. 'Put that down,' he yelled.

She dropped the board in surprise.

'Haven't you got an ounce of sense?' he yelled.

'But you said——'

'I don't care what I said! I don't want any injuries on this job. If you can't do something, just admit it. What are you, part bulldog?'

'I can do it.' That little chin was starting to point skywards.

'Have you ever heard the word humility?'

'I'm surprised that's a word you're familiar with,' she returned.

'Look, squirt, you're five feet two and weigh about ninety-six pounds. You can't lift the joists. They weigh nearly as much as you do.'

'Then why did you ask me to do it in the first place?'

To prove you couldn't do it. That niggle of shame came back. 'I was being a jerk.'

She stared at him. Her lips, those aggravating lips, which were naturally full of colour and shaped just like kissable little bows, began to twitch. A sparkle that was not anger came into the green-gold of her eyes. She snorted, trying to hold it in, but she couldn't.

She laughed. It was like hearing water bubbling, clear and lovely, over rocks.

He watched her stonily. She looked beautiful. Free and natural. Lord, he wanted this woman off his house. But not bad enough to have crippling her on his conscience.

'Do you know how to handle a Skilsaw?'

A little smile teased her lips. Dammit. He'd walked right into a trap. This was the moment she'd been waiting for.

Over the next hour, he saw she knew how to measure, and how to use the saw. Things began to clip along at the speed he liked. He'd tried to show Moose, over the years, how to do some of the thinking on a project, instead of just the donkey work, but his instructions had never quite penetrated the thickness of Moose's skull.

He turned and looked at Moose. Over the years, it had become a habit. Check and yell. Moose could be found gazing off into the distance, or might have disappeared somewhere for a smoke, or would be working away at a contented snail's pace.

He frowned when he saw him now. Working. Really working. Moose was sweating! Blaze's eyes narrowed. Every now and then Moose slid the little shrimp a look— to see if she was noticing him!

He was showing off for her! All these wasted years, Blaze thought with grim humour. A woman on the site was just what was needed. He'd never seen Moose put out like that.

'Hey, Clarence,' he called.

Moose looked up, startled.

'Nice work.' He'd never seen Clarence smile like that before. It kind of reminded him of a neglected dog who'd been patted on the head. He felt that little squeeze of shame again. Hell! If he'd wanted to explore the puzzles of human nature he would have got a job in social work or something disgustingly humanitarian like that.

If he didn't get rid of that woman she was going to wind up teaching him all sorts of things about himself that he'd spent years of utter contentment not knowing.

Janey was aware of him, all the time. It was a deeply disturbing feeling. She had not had this same awareness of Jonathan when they had worked together.

Of course, a dentist's office was civilised and businesslike. There was nothing 'physical' happening, really. People didn't sweat there, and they certainly didn't remove their shirts. The atmosphere in dental offices did not lend itself to primal thoughts the way this environment did. There was a certain rawness on a building site that stripped away façades, rather than helping them stay in place.

And, of course, Jonathan was not quite the male specimen that Blaze Hamilton was, though the very admission made her feel disloyal. Still, it was true. The pure power of Blaze was mesmerising. It stirred something deeply disturbing in her, watching the play of work-hardened muscles beneath his T-shirt and jeans.

He wasn't her type, of course, any more than Clarence was. And yet she was aware of him in a way she was not aware of Clarence. It made her feel like a traitor, being so physically aware of the man who had engineered her father's downfall. Especially since she was engaged to a man who couldn't be more different from Blaze Hamilton.

Maybe, she thought wryly, I should have taken up social work, where I could have studied the puzzles of human behaviour. No, it was nothing that puzzling. It was nature, pure and simple. Biology, not psychology. The female naturally drawn to the most domineering, fittest member of her species.

Thank goodness human beings had brains and souls to balance those biological urges, and to keep them from getting into all kinds of trouble. She slid him one more look. Because that man was trouble wearing tight jeans.

With determination, she drew her *full* attention back to the blueprint, studied it for a moment, measured and cut the next piece of plywood.

She smiled as the smell of sawdust teased her nostrils, and then shivered as she watched Blaze pull a joist from the heap, snap it on to his shoulder, and toss it on to the floor. He wrestled it easily over to where he wanted it, slammed a nail into it with two blows of his hammer. The air nailer was sitting beside him, but he ignored it, banging home the next two nails with awe-inspiring ease.

She felt the quiver of shocked appreciation of him down to her belly. *Biology*, she reminded herself firmly.

She turned away, lifted the piece of plywood she had just cut and carried it over to where it fitted in the floor. She set it down and shoved it into place with her foot.

She had the oddest sensation of the floor moving, swaying beneath her. Of course, buildings did have a bit of sway until all the pieces were put together. Shrugging it off, she turned to go back to the saw.

And then felt that sensation of movement again. She glanced around uncertainly. She knew she was in trouble when she saw the look on Blaze's face. The normal schooled cynicism of those handsome features had been replaced by horrified shock.

He wasn't sure what made him turn and look towards her—some odd feeling of something off just a touch— a vague perception of movement just caught out of the corner of his eye.

The floor was moving!

'Run!' he shouted.

But she stood there on the swaying floor like a sailor on a storm-tossed ship.

'Move!' he shouted again, but she was like a deer mesmerised by the lights of a vehicle, staring at the heaving floor with a kind of dazed bewilderment in her eyes.

He was already running when he hit the moving section of the floor. The sway was becoming violent; he could barely keep his balance. But nothing could have stopped him. He charged across the shifting lumber towards her.

He reached her. He grabbed her wrist, and tugged her towards him with more violence than he realised. She smashed into his chest. He grabbed her around the waist, registering a stupid, silly detail, as the mind sometimes did in a crisis. His big hands very nearly spanned the narrowness of her waist. He picked her up, part of his mind again sifting slowly through unnecessary information. She was light as a feather, and soft in all the right places.

If his mind was working slowly, in fragments, his body was not. He tossed her over his shoulder and ran with lightning speed towards solid ground.

Why wasn't the whole house collapsing? his mind asked lazily. Would the other section start to collapse just as he reached it? Dammit! Why did she smell like lemons and dewdrops mixed together?

The floor was moaning, an unearthly sound. And then with a shrieking creak it began to collapse right behind him. Using every ounce of his strength he jumped for the stable floor, aware that he was now leaping through space, the floor and the joists sliding out from underneath him.

His landing was jarring. He pitched forward, and instead of letting her go he held her tighter. A mistake. She hit the floor with a bone crunching whack, on her back. The full force of his own weight came crashing down on top of her.

He rolled off her almost instantly, feeling like a bear who had crushed a wild flower, and suddenly feeling dazed and sluggish himself.

The silence was unearthly, dirt and sawdust rising in a cloud from where the floor had given in. And then the silence was broken by the tiny sound of her gasping for breath.

Or at first he thought she was gasping for breath. He looked at her and then he realised she was crying.

He lifted himself up to a sitting position and looked awkwardly at her lying there, on her back, staring up at the sky with that same bewildered look, only now tears were clouding the usual clearness of those enormous gold-green eyes, sliding off thick lashes, and creating furrows in the sawdust that dusted her cheeks.

'Hell,' he muttered. He tried to think what to do. He had an 'A' grade Industrial First Aid certificate. He should know what to do. But his mind had slowed down again, was flashing one message at him over and over so that he couldn't think of anything else.

Hold her.

He scooped her up, and held her against him. Her cheek nestled in the crook of his neck. Her cheek was soft and velvety, like the petal on a rose. One of her teardrops chased down his shirt through the tangle of hair on his chest. She was trembling like a kitten who'd been forgotten out in a storm. Her curls tickled his nose, and that morning-fresh smell of lemons and dew enveloped him.

'Hell,' he said again, more softly.

'What happened, boss? Is Janey hurt?'

The voice jarred him. For a frozen moment it had seemed as if they were two survivors washed up on a desert island.

He looked up to see Moose and Tuffy staring at the wrecked floor in amazement. And then at him. And her. With even more amazement.

Blaze practically threw her in his effort to get out from under the soft, sweet weight of her as quickly as possible. He set her down and lunged to his feet.

'I don't think so.' He glared at her. 'Are you hurt?' If he had done that on his first-aid exam they wouldn't have given him a certificate to look at injured mosquitoes.

'No, I'm——' her voice broke '—fine,' she finished weakly, wiping frantically at her tears with the back of her sleeve.

Normally, he would have checked her thoroughly for breaks or bruises. But nothing was normal. The world seemed to be tilting crazily, only this time it had nothing to do with the floor. And he couldn't touch her any more than he already had without reacting in an embarrassing way. Hell! Women!

He took a deep steadying breath.

'What happened?' Moose asked again.

'I don't know what the hell happened,' he snapped. But what had happened was as good a way as any of diverting his attention from her, still huddled on the floor, still hurting, looking for all the world like a kid who had fallen off a bicycle.

Except he did not get these ridiculous uncontrollable urges from kids. Or bicycles, for that matter.

He decided he was in shock, too. Not thinking rationally, his brain shut down, *completely*.

What happened? he reminded himself.

He didn't know what had happened to his house, and he didn't know what had happened to him when he was holding that soft, sweet-smelling piece of fluff in his arms. But he knew that, whatever it was, it spelled disaster all the way around.

He walked over to the edge of the unharmed floor and stared down at the wreckage of fallen joists and broken plywood. He allowed himself a moment of gratitude that no one had been seriously hurt. That she hadn't been seriously hurt. But only one moment. Then he scowled. In all his days as a builder he had never seen anything like this. He'd never even heard of anything like this happening. What would make a floor collapse?

He turned and stalked past the others. Moose was swatting Janey on the shoulder in an obvious effort to be comforting, and looking bloody self-conscious about it, too. Tuffy was squatting on his heels, his face impassive. Janey was sitting up, her head resting on her knees.

'You're probably about to hear some words you ain't never heard before,' he warned Janey protectively as Blaze moved by them.

Blaze grunted, and felt dim approval for Tuffy. Now there was a man who knew how he was supposed to act— equally unmoved by crises and feminine snivelling. Casting Janey one more look that was a combination of bitter resentment and the concern that caused the bitter resentment, he leaped off the side of the house and into the soft dirt surrounding it.

Janey gave Clarence a weak smile. She wished he would stop pounding on her shoulder, but she didn't have the heart to rebuff his attempts at comforting her. She didn't look as Blaze stomped off the floor. A moment later, they could hear him down there, sifting violently through materials.

She still felt shocked. And not just by the accident either, but by the warm security she had felt in the arms of Blaze Hamilton! By how the smell of him, masculine and strong and earthy, had filled her with comfort, how the steady beat of his heart had filled her with an almost sleepy contentment. The hard strength of him as he held her had chased away the fear she had experienced, and even the pain in her back where she had landed on the floor.

'Moose, Tuffy, get down here. Now!'

They exchanged looks. Janey struggled to her feet.

'You don't have to,' Moose told her gruffly.

'I'm OK.' Actually, she felt as if she had been slowly rolled over by a sixteen-ton steamroller. Gingerly she tested each of her limbs. Nothing broken, only battered, her physical self mirroring her emotional one.

'You don't want to be round Blaze when he's like this.'

'I can handle it,' she said proudly. She had to handle it! It was bad enough that she had cried—no doubt a first on a Hamilton construction site. She couldn't follow that with being overly sensitive to his mood, which was going to be about as black as black could get unless she missed her guess.

Moose shrugged, with an obvious lack of conviction. She followed him off the ladder and down to basement level.

'Start clearing this up,' Blaze barked without looking at them. She watched the play of his broad back as he heaved broken material out of the hole. If he could channel that temper, she thought bemusedly, he could win Olympic titles.

'And look for the tele-post. When I find that defective piece of crap, I'll——'

He stopped, whirled, and glowered at her. She wasn't sure how he even knew she was there, though his nostrils were flaring like a wolf who had caught scent of something on the wind.

'Are you all right?'

The words were harsh, and she felt herself flinch away from them, yearning for the gentle concern she had felt when he had lifted her into the warm haven of his lap, the protective circle of his arms.

But that was unrealistic. All that had been unreal, and now they were firmly back in reality.

'I think so.'

'If you don't *know*, I'll have somebody drive you over to the hospital just to be sure.'

And it wouldn't be him driving her from the hard, cold anger in each word. Why was he angry? Because he'd been caught in an unguarded moment of tenderness? With one of his crew?

'Why are you angry?' she said, folding her arms over her chest.

'My house just caved in,' he said, putting enough expletives in between 'my' and 'house' to impress the entire marine corps. 'Maybe I should be dancing?'

But she was certain the anger went deeper than that, not that she wanted to push it.

'I don't need to go to the hospital. I'm fine.'

'You don't look "fine". You're about the same colour as my aunt Matilda's hair—white with a little blue around the edges. I've had enough accidents for today. If you're going to faint go somewhere else to do it.'

'I'm just shaken,' she said stubbornly. 'And I never faint.'

'And I never have buildings fall down. There's a first time for everything.'

'I won't faint,' she repeated resolutely.

'Good, because generally when I have a woman in my arms it isn't to give her mouth-to-mouth, and I plan to keep it that way.' He said that with the grim determination of a man who had decided never to touch her again, no matter what.

'If I did faint, I'd rather hit the floor than be rescued by you, anyway. But I won't. I don't even feel that shaken any more.' Just good and miffed by his male arrogance!

'Then get to work. You think I'm paying you ten bucks an hour to stand around and feel sorry for yourself?'

'I am not feeling sorry for myself!' she gasped with indignation.

'Well, you're not working either, are you?'

It wasn't as if she hadn't been warned, she thought with sudden wry insight. Moose had told her she wouldn't like being around him.

He was in a miserable temper. She could see the tension knotted in the muscles of his shoulders, the tension clenched in his hands.

'Blaze?'

'What now?'

'Thank you,' she said sweetly.

'For what?'

'For pulling me off the floor. You might have saved my life.'

'I doubt it,' he said gruffly. 'I might have saved you a broken bone or two. And something else—I wouldn't have done that for a man! I would have let him get himself out of that mess.'

She met his gaze levelly. 'Sure.'

'Shows what you know. Now get to work.'

Slowly they cleared the joists and plywood out of the basement area. There was surprisingly little damage—a few sheets of broken plywood, and a whole lot of twisted nails.

But there was no tele-post—the metal cylinder that supported the main beam, and eventually took the weight of the whole house on it. Most houses had three of these, but this house, because of its size, had six. The other tele-posts were in place, which explained why only a section of the floor had collapsed.

'Moose, Tuff, go have lunch. You,' he snapped at Janey, 'stay here.'

She had known this was coming, and she braced herself. They stood staring at each other in the semi-darkness of the basement.

'You were supposed to do the tele-posts,' he stated quietly.

The features of his handsome face were no longer animated by anger. They had turned to cold, rock-hard stone.

'I did them, Blaze.'

'You did five of them.'

'I did six of them.'

'If you'd done six of them, I wouldn't have a house coming down around my ears. If you made a mistake, admit it. I made a mistake myself. I should have checked to make sure they were done and done right.'

'I did them,' she said stubbornly.

'Then why did the house fall down?'

'I don't have a clue,' she said. She could not back down from the flat, dangerous light in his eyes. If she did it was all over right now. And it was for nothing. 'Maybe you want to get rid of me even worse than I thought.'

That colour was rising up from his neck again. 'What are you saying?'

'That this is a mistake you could legitimately fire someone for, isn't it?'

'You take that back,' he said, with soft menace. 'As if I would endanger people's lives to get rid of a little chit like you. That would be the equivalent of dropping an A-bomb on a gnat.'

'Maybe you had other motives,' she said mulishly.

'Like what?' he said with menace so lethal she should have backed away from it.

'How about insurance? Is your insurance going to cover this?'

He snorted, a sound like a bull before a charge. 'You better start apologising, and quick.'

'It doesn't feel very wonderful to be blamed for something you didn't do, does it, Blaze?' She backed away from her accusation quickly. She realised she didn't want Blaze to know she suspected him of any kind of impropriety.

'Oh, hell—feelings. I don't have any, and I don't care about yours. At this moment all I want to know is why this house came down—and I sure as hell know I didn't do it!'

'I put in the posts.'

'The evidence says you didn't.'

'There is no evidence.' And suddenly she knew that that was the missing piece. The awareness seemed to dawn in his face, too, a puzzled expression furrowing his brow, as he turned and scanned the hole again for the missing post.

'Where the hell is that sixth post?' he mused. 'I know we brought six of them down here yesterday.'

'That's right. Five of them are up. If I forgot, the sixth one should be lying around here somewhere. Where is it?'

He blinked. 'That's a good question,' he admitted. He looked up and inspected the sagging beam. He suddenly didn't look angry, or dangerous any more. Just weary to the bone. Absently he ran a powerful hand through the springy sun-streaked lightness of his hair.

'There are nail holes here where the anchor was.' His voice was a low growl. 'Maybe I made a mistake.'

'Maybe?' she pressed.

He scowled at her. 'For someone so little, you sure are pushy, aren't you? OK, I was upset and I started throwing accusations around. Maybe some kids got in here last night and took the post. I don't know what happened.'

'I'm sorry, too,' she said reluctantly.

'Aw, get out of here. Go eat your lunch.'

Moose was eating his lunch when she came up out of the hole. He slid her a wary look.

'Do you still work here?' he finally asked.

'I guess so,' she said without much enthusiasm.

'Blaze is just blowing off steam. Don't worry about him. Mistakes happen.'

'I didn't do it!'

'Oh.'

'Blaze thinks maybe some kids . . . last night.'

Moose brightened. 'That could be. 'Cos the post ain't even down there anywhere, is it?'

'No. Has anything like this ever happened before?' She wasn't really in the mood to play detective, but she had to remind herself she was here for a reason, and this might be her first lead—though Blaze had been believable enough when she'd asked him about insurance.

'Nah. Blaze is a real stickler for safety.'

That didn't sound like somebody who would cut corners, either.

She ate her sandwich in weary silence. Blaze Hamilton was baffling. He was also unreasonable, unbearably stubborn, too quick to jump to conclusions, too hot-tempered, and entirely unfair.

But the man had saved her life this morning. She was fairly certain of that, even if he had tried to brush it off.

She just couldn't find it in her to hate him right now.

The hospital was quiet, ceiling lights reflecting brightly off the highly polished hallway floor. Janey hesitated outside room 301 West, and then, taking a deep breath, pushed.

He had some pillows propped up behind his back, and was sitting up, but his eyes were closed. Tubes went in his nose and he was hooked on to an intravenous. His face had that awful grey pallor still, and he looked so thin and frail.

It seemed to her that there was only a shadow of her father there, a shadow of the big robust man with the loud laugh who had been so full of energy and strength.

'Hi, Dad.' She touched his arm.

His eyes opened and he smiled wanly. 'Janey, love.' His voice was a mere whisper. His eyes looked tired and without sparkle.

She didn't stay long. She could tell even her brief visit was straining his stamina. A man who could once hammer nails and heft materials for ten hours a day was now strained by saying hello!

She left feeling cheated. Where was the man her father used to be? Would they ever have him back?

It was Blaze Hamilton's fault he was like this. He'd saved her life today, but did that mean he could be absolved for the part he had played in killing her father? If she could somehow reverse what had happened eight years ago, would her father start to come back?

She had been so aware tonight that her father was a dying man. She had been so aware that only a miracle could save him. Could Blaze Hamilton's being brought to justice after all these years provide that miraculous impetus for her father to start getting well? For him to at least find the will to go on? Tonight he had seemed like a man so utterly defeated, and she hated that. She hated feeling she had no control over this situation.

She *needed* to get Blaze Hamilton.

She needed to believe he had caused the accident this morning himself, for some gain she didn't yet understand.

But she would. She swore she would.

CHAPTER FOUR

'JANEY! No!'

She had been about to step up on a sawhorse. The tone of Blaze's voice stopped her in her tracks—the tone of his voice and the fact he had actually used her name.

She turned and gave him a cursory look. He was stalking across the floor towards her, his face like thunder.

It turned out that his interest was in the sawhorse. Fascinated, she watched him pick it up, swear, and snap a leg off it as if it were a toothpick. Her jaw fell open.

He saw her expression and a reluctant grin broke through the fierce cast of his features.

'That wasn't quite as impressive as it looked.' He snapped off another one.

It looked pretty darned impressive!

His good humour disappeared as quickly as it had arrived. He scowled. 'Look.'

He handed her the sawhorse, and she inspected one of the remaining legs.

The legs looked fine, but on close inspection she could see the line of a saw. The leg had been cut clear through, and was virtually hanging by a thread. She snapped it off herself. Neither of them smiled.

'Moose nearly killed himself on one of these when he came in this morning.'

'One of them?' she echoed.

'It wasn't until I saw you heading for this one that I realised that they might all be booby-trapped.'

'Someone could have been seriously hurt,' she said slowly.

'Yeah.' He flung the broken sawhorse off the side of the house, and strode over to the next one. He snapped the legs off it as if they too were toothpicks.

She watched him uncertainly. What was going on with this house? Blaze seemed authentically perturbed by this incident. Besides, what on earth would he have to gain by an injury to his own workers?

'Who do you think did this?' she asked.

'Kids, I guess,' he said, but he didn't sound very convinced. Someone had taken a little more time with those sawhorses than a mere prank was worth.

Still, she had come here to find inconsistencies, and she was finding them. They didn't have to make any sense at the moment. Sometimes incomprehensible little things all came together to make a very understandable big picture.

Maybe he was going to burn his own house down later, or something like that, and blame it on those same 'kids'. He'd have plenty of witnesses to the ongoing incidents of vandalism.

Blaze glanced back at Janey. She was wearing a yellow T-shirt today, a man's, at least three sizes too large for her. She had it tucked into a pair of faded jeans that weren't in the least large, and it was an appealing sight. Add to that the faint tan that was giving her skin a golden glow despite her religious application of sunscreen, and the freckles that were darkening across the bridge of her perky little nose, and it was a fairly attractive combination.

What was not attractive was the look in her eyes as she watched him. She looked angry. Accusing.

He looked back at her with open challenge. She looked away. But somehow he could not get the frustrated fury in her eyes out of his mind.

He needed a number of things from his storage yard, and suddenly replacing those sawhorses seemed imperative. He could also think of several errands downtown that suddenly seemed urgent.

He tossed the last vandalised sawhorse savagely off the side of the house. He had an enemy, it would seem. He looked at Janey's rigid back. More than one, maybe.

He sighed. He supposed that was what came of a lifetime pursuit of freedom from diplomacy.

An hour later Blaze climbed back out of his truck, and retrieved the replacement sawhorses from the box. He paused and looked up the hill. He was behind schedule, but he supposed that was to be expected after the floor had collapsed.

Things looked not too bad. Though it was fast approaching the lunch-hour, they were still working. He felt pleasantly surprised by that. Moose only continued to work as long as he'd made sure to assign what to do next. If he ran out of things Blaze had told him to do, Blaze would return from picking up supplies or running errands to find him stretched out unapologetically in the sun.

But they were all working. Janey and Moose were bent over... He squinted.

'My Skilsaw!' he yelped, and bolted up the hill. 'What do you think you're doing?' he yelled, yanking the plug out of the cord before they could do any damage.

Janey turned and looked at him. He remembered why he had left—because of a loose yellow T-shirt, and jeans that weren't loose at all. Because of skin faintly tanned from the mild September sun, and freckles scattering across her nose.

Because when she turned those green-gold eyes on him they were full of anger.

He didn't know how he'd finally succeeded in making her angry; he only knew he wished it would go away. It was bad enough that he couldn't get rid of her.

'What the hell are you doing?' he snapped.

'I'm teaching Clarence how to measure and use the saw.'

'Well, forget it. I've already tried and three Skilsaws is about all I'm willing to invest in furthering Moose's education.'

'How do you break a Skilsaw?' she asked incredulously.

'Let's see. Once he cut through the cord. No, *twice* he cut through the cord, and the other time I don't precisely remember what happened, but I do remember it cost me money.'

The pipsqueak looked disgusted with *him*.

'Here,' she said, plugging the cord back in. 'Let me just show you.' She handed the Skilsaw back to Moose.

'I don't want to do it with him here,' Moose said sullenly.

Blaze felt his mouth drop open. 'I happen to be the guy who signs your pay-cheque, not her. If you can do something, show me.'

'You make me nervous,' Moose said, looking stubbornly at the toe of his big work boot.

'I make you nervous?' Blaze bellowed. 'I didn't make you nervous a week ago!' He looked daggers at Janey. This was her doing.

'It makes me nervous when you start yelling. That's why I cut the cords. That's why I don't do anything unless you're here, 'cos if I do it wrong you yell and throw things.'

Blaze looked incredulously at the man who towered over him. *He* made Moose nervous?

'Janey makes it easy to understand when she shows me how to do something, and she doesn't get mad if I do it wrong.'

'Because it's not her money going down the drain when you do it wrong!'

'Money is always the bottom line, isn't it?' she said, and it was everything he could do not to flinch from the distaste in her voice.

'As a matter of fact, yes,' he snapped, 'and if you'll sign this I'll have some more of it. The government's going to pay half your wages.' He shoved the paper he'd picked up downtown at her. In his anxiety over his saw it had somehow become quite crumpled.

She took it, carefully straightened it out, asked him for a pen and signed it. When she leaned over the sun glinted in her hair and made it look like liquid honey.

'If the government's paying you half, you can afford to give me more.' She handed the paper back to him.

Geez, she was quick. He felt trapped. She'd just accused him of making money the bottom line, and now she was gathering evidence.

'Has anybody ever told you you're pushy? You don't spend a week on a job and then start hinting for a raise.'

'I wasn't hinting. I told you from the beginning I was worth twelve.'

Dammit, she *was* worth twelve. Not on the bull work, but you didn't pay somebody twelve dollars an hour to do bull work, anyway.

If he gave her a raise, he'd probably never get rid of her. That faint scent of lemons came and tickled his nostrils.

'We'll have a look at it at the end of the month—if you're still around.'

'I'll be around.'

'Why? You can't be having fun working for a mean old cheapskate like me.'

'Fun isn't everything.'

He didn't like the way she said that. He could see the softness in the woman. There was a sweetness in her eyes and a gentleness in the way she talked to Moose. But when she turned her attention on him she was as hard as a keg of nails.

He supposed he deserved it. And he didn't care. Hell, had he ever cared what anybody who worked for him thought of him? Which was another of his crimes, according to her.

That scent came to him again, mingled with the sunshine, and the colour of her hair and the way her jeans fitted.

'You,' he said to Janey, 'can go down to Harvey's Hardware and pick up a couple of skyhooks, so we can lift the walls. Take the truck.'

'What's a skyhook?'

It's a way of getting rid of you for the afternoon. 'One of the few technical advances in this trade. A relatively new invention. An inverse force pulley. What do you want? A picture? Just go get the things, on the double.'

'Yessir,' she muttered under her breath.

He tossed the keys at her, and she caught them. He watched her go, his eyes involuntarily drawn to the sweet curve of her rear end.

The truck roared away, probably leaving black tyre tracks for three feet. All he could think, was, Good, the faster you're out of my sight the better.

'Aw, boss,' Moose said, 'why are you going to pull that on her?'

'You've always thought it was funny before,' Blaze reminded him blackly.

Moose considered that. 'Yeah, it is pretty funny.' He grinned and it made that monster of a man look about ten years old.

'Look, Moose,' Blaze said uncomfortably, 'Clarence, I know I haven't got the greatest people skills. I have a low frustration level. I don't have enough patience to teach people how to do things right. I want it done, I want it done now, and I want it perfect, so I end up doing it myself.'

'I know that, boss.'

'I'm just trying to say I never meant to make you nervous. Hell, I just thought it slid off your back. Usually I'm just blowing off steam.'

'That's OK, boss.' Moose clapped him on the shoulder with unexpected gentleness.

Damn, Blaze thought, we're turning into raving namby-pambies. He turned abruptly away from Moose but not before he saw the loyalty and liking in his over-sized employee's face. He felt far more touched than he wanted to.

'OK, get on that south wall. I want it up by——'

He moved away and glanced over at Tuffy. Tuffy just worked. He didn't talk, he didn't complain, he didn't even ask questions. He just did what was expected of him, day in and day out, and collected his pay cheque as silently as he had earned it. In the three years he'd worked for Blaze, he might have said three words.

Thank goodness.

'Hey, Tuff, good work,' Blaze said gruffly to him.

Tuffy didn't even look up, just grunted.

Good man, Blaze thought with relief. Damn that Janey Smith right to hell. He wasn't running an etiquette emporium. Well, he was going to have the last laugh today.

Janey walked into Harvey's Hardware. She liked the smell of hardware stores, and she lingered purposefully in the doorway for a moment. She wasn't going slow, but she wasn't rushing either. She was in no rush to get back to that man. Who smelled like sunshine and soap and sweat. Who had that lion's mane of white-gold hair. Who had skin the colour of polished copper that the sweat beaded on in tiny diamond drops. Who had muscles so sleek and hard that he could have been a statue cast from steel.

'Yes, ma'am, can I help you?' the bald man in the plaid shirt asked her.

Who was loud and rude and insensitive and probably crooked to boot, she told herself. She sternly pulled her attention away from the man she had not managed to get away from after all and focused on the less awe-inspiring male specimen behind the counter.

'I'm from Hamilton's Construction. Blaze needs a couple of skyhooks.'

'Durn it all, I'm right out of them. Won't have any
for a week. But Blaze has an account at Big Bend
Builder's, too. You might try over there.'

She tried Big Bend and Kelly's and the Hardware
Emporium. It was the clerk at Hardware Emporium that
gave it away.

'Hey, Mike,' he called to his co-worker, 'Blaze
Hamilton sent over for some skyhooks. Got any skyhooks back there?'

She heard the stifled snort, was aware of a head poking
out from the back of the shop to inspect her, and more
stifled snorts before a barely controlled voice called back,
'Nope, seem to be all out of them today.'

'He's having me on, isn't he?' she deduced, feeling
indignant anger begin to burn deep within her. He hadn't
been able to physically grind her into the ground, so now
he was going to try and humiliate her.

Some day she hoped she would be sitting in front of
a packed-to-the-rafters courtroom telling them all what
a villain he was. His building collapsed. The legs fell off
his sawhorses. He sent me for skyhooks when no such
thing exists.

The clerk laughed. 'Yeah, he's having you on. He does
it to all his rookies.'

Janey's anger died an abrupt death. He did it to all
his rookies? Blaze had a sense of humour? Blaze used
paid time to play jokes on people?

The significance of it dawned on her, and filled her
with such unexpected warmth that the courtroom scene
was completely obliterated from her imagination. Blaze
probably didn't even realise the significance of it himself,
or he wouldn't have done it. But in a twisted kind of
way he had just accepted her.

She smiled broadly at the clerk. 'What would you say a skyhook would be worth?'

The clerk looked puzzled. 'That's the joke. There's no such thing.'

'But if there were such a thing, what do you think it would be worth?'

He began to get her drift. 'A small fortune,' he said solemnly. He pulled out his billing book. 'How about four of them at a thousand dollars a piece?'

'Sounds good to me,' she said, watching him make out the bogus bill with great care.

'I wish I could be there to see his face,' he said with a big grin when he ripped the bill off his pad and handed it to her.

Janey parked the truck, hopped out and dashed up the hill. Blaze came towards her, slipping the big framing hammer into his apron without even looking for the slot.

'Where the hell have you been?' he snapped. 'Did you get them? You've been holding up production all afternoon.'

She made her face every bit as serious as his, though she could see the twinkle of suppressed mirth that turned the blue of his eyes to winking star sapphires.

She passed him the envelope. 'They've had a real run on them. I had to order them, but they'll be delivered first thing tomorrow.'

She saw Moose pause in what he was doing, and shuffle a little closer. Even Tuffy's hammer stopped mid-swing. But it was Blaze she focused on, his brows knit into a fine frown as he tore open the envelope.

He pulled out the slip of paper and scanned it. She watched as the thunder clouds began to build in the clear blue of those eyes.

'Four thousand dollars! For what?' he exploded.

'Skyhooks,' she responded innocently. 'Isn't that what you wanted? I could have sworn that's what you asked for. Inverse force pulleys to help lift the walls, right?'

'What the hell have you done? What did you buy?'

She gauged carefully how long to let him suffer. She was aware of the absolute stillness as both Tuffy and Clarence waited for him to blow up. His hand shoved back the sun-streaked hair from his forehead as he looked again at the bill.

His eyes narrowed to flashing midnight-blue slits. He opened his mouth. Tuffy and Clarence braced themselves.

'The last laugh,' she told him, quietly, before he could speak. 'I bought the last laugh.'

Then she took the bill from him, and tore it into little pieces and let them scatter on the wind.

Moose laughed first, and then even Tuffy gave a few rusty-sounding cackles of amusement.

Blaze stared at her. She saw the light of laughter spark in his eyes, and then a twitch disturbed the stern line around his lips. His shoulders started to shake. And then he threw back his head and laughed. His laughter was a deep and joy-filled rumble; he laughed with the same intensity with which he worked, giving himself completely over to his enjoyment. She laughed then, too. All of them laughed.

Even when the laughter had subsided, the good feeling twinkled in the air, like stardust, around them.

Blaze gave her shoulder a light punch that would almost have to be called affectionate. But the jolt of pure electricity she felt was too raw to be associated with anything so tame as mere affection.

'Get back to work, Smith. You've wasted enough of my time.'

'And you,' she shot back, 'have wasted enough of mine.'

The sharp words did not make the twinkle go away, nor the current that throbbed almost painfully, running the length of her arm to her heart.

And it was then she was aware that something bad had just happened. She was aware that for a split-second she had liked Blaze Hamilton, very, very much.

'Blaze, honey.'

Janey whirled. A tall, curvaceous woman with beautiful long, tousled blonde hair was leaning out of the door of a midnight-blue sports car. She was wearing a flame-coloured sundress that was high at the thigh and low at the bosom. She looked like a model for flashy cars, warm places, or expensive jewellery.

'I said get to work,' Blaze repeated.

Janey felt the red creep up her cheeks. What on earth was she doing gawking at Blaze's...what? Sister? Not likely. Secretary? Ha. It was Blaze's romantic interest, and she did not know why her stomach suddenly had a hard anxious knot in it.

She went to work on the south wall, working beside Clarence. Every now and then she carefully slid her eyes over to the car, where Blaze and the woman were talking.

'She's a looker, ain't she?' Moose said, surprising Janey by seeing exactly where her covert glances were going.

'Stunning,' Janey agreed with a flatness that did not entirely disguise her envy.

'Beauty's only skin deep,' Clarence said, and the gentle loyalty in his voice almost brought tears to her eyes. 'Blaze always has great-looking girlfriends.'

'Does he have many girlfriends?' She tried to sound only casually interested.

'The ladies are crazy about him.'

I don't care if he has a harem, she told herself fiercely.

'But he doesn't seem to much notice the kind of attention he stirs up.'

Now that did not fit in with the image she wanted to have of him. Greedy. Callous. Egotistical. Macho.

'He usually has a girlfriend, but at the stage you'd think he'd be thinking about getting hitched he's usually trying to figure out how to get rid of them.'

That was better. Heart-breaking monster. Getting rid of the women who had given him the best years of their lives as if they were so much furniture! *Lady-killer*, she mentally added to his list of crimes.

'He always picks women who are sup-er-fic-ial.' Clarence struggled with every syllable of that word and then beamed proudly when he managed to get it out.

Janey frowned at Clarence. She didn't want him taking the blame for the broken relationships off Blaze.

'Blaze is a real nice guy——'

Oh, sure, for a heart-breaking monster.

'But he seems to pick women who kind of take advantage of him.'

That turned her version around so completely that Janey had no choice but to laugh at her own absurdity.

'My, it certainly looks like you're having fun today,' Melanie commented.

'We just played a joke on the rookie.' He looked at Melanie appreciatively. Lord, she was one good-looking woman.

'What was it?'

He explained skyhooks to her. She didn't laugh. She looked faintly puzzled. He decided not to tell her about the counterfeit bill Janey had had made up.

'I dropped by because I forgot to get you to sign this cheque this morning.'

'What cheque?'

'Remember you said you would pay for that dress I liked at the Glass Unicorn?'

'Oh, yeah.' He signed the cheque she passed him. He didn't remember saying that at all.

'It's the pink one I told you about. I thought I'd get a tiny gold bracelet to go with it. I don't think I'll need a new necklace, though, I...'

No wonder he couldn't remember. Already, he found his attention drifting. Back up the rise to the house. Janey was hammering a stud into place. She was getting good with the hammer, the rhythm of it hitting the nail deep and even. He heard the low-pitched rumble of Moose's voice, and then the tinkle of Janey's laughter. It was an unexpected sound, gentle against the hard sounds of hammers and saws and men's voices. It was like hearing a bird sing in a war zone.

Melanie stopped talking mid-sentence, turned and squinted up the hill. At that moment Janey was walking across the floor with a freshly cut stud. There was no mistaking the feminine swing of her walk. Melanie turned and stared at him, her look cold and hard.

'That's not a boy. That's a girl.'

'You're partly right,' he replied flatly. 'It's a woman.' He couldn't believe that decidedly feminist correction had come from his mouth. He vowed to wash it out with soap as soon as he could.

'Your rookie is a woman?'

Fight time, he thought, taking in the narrowed eyes, noting the faint shrillness that had clung to that last word.

He folded his arms over his chest. 'So?'

'So you might have told me before.'

'You've never been interested in what happens here before.'

'Don't make it sound like I'm not interested in your work.'

'You're not.'

'Blaze, you're trying to skirt the issue here.'

The issue was skirts all right, he thought drily. 'The issue is that my business is my business. It has never concerned you before, and it doesn't concern you now.'

'I don't want her working here.'

For some reason he didn't feel inclined to tell Melanie he had shared precisely that sentiment for over a week.

'Oh?' he invited, hoping she would catch from his tone that she was on very dicey ground.

She didn't. 'Blaze, I want you to get rid of her. I want you to get rid of her right now. And that's my final word.'

'Your final word,' he repeated incredulously. For some reason he felt that Melanie should have figured out by now that the wrong way to approach an issue with him was to be snapping out orders.

'A *girl* on a construction site. That's absolutely the last thing I want to see when I come and visit you at work.'

He could not believe how oblivious she was to his body language, how completely immersed she was in herself. In eight months she had probably visited him at work three times. Briefly. With a chequebook.

'I'm not particularly interested in what you want to see happening on my construction site,' he told her. Somehow, just barely, he was keeping the leash on his temper, but he knew his voice came out colder than an arctic wind.

She backed off instantly, a pout replacing the anger around her red-painted mouth. 'It's just not right. It's kind of...weird.'

'Weird,' he repeated dangerously. 'It's weird for a woman to work like a son-of-a-gun to earn her living, but not for a man?'

'When did you become a feminist?'

About three seconds ago. He'd be the guest speaker at their meetings next, if he didn't watch himself.

'She works hard. She knows what she's doing. That's all that matters to me.' A thousand wild horses wouldn't make him say that to *her*, though.

'I don't like it, Blaze. I don't like it at all.'

'Why don't *you* come out here and work for me for a couple of days?' he said silkily. 'It would do you good to understand how I make that money you're so eager to spend. You'd understand me better. I think I'd understand you better, too.'

'Have you lost your ever-loving mind?' she hissed.

He looked at her. 'She does it.'

Melanie snorted with disgust. 'She probably drinks beer and burps, too.'

He felt a surge of protective and outraged anger that took him completely off guard. That kind of scared him, if truth be known.

'As far as I can tell, Janey's a class act.'

'A woman carpenter who is a class act?' Melanie sneered. 'You wouldn't know class if it stepped on you, Blaze Hamilton.'

'So you've been telling me for several months now,' he said tightly.

Again, she knew she'd gone too far, and her anger melted into a kittenish expression of hurt. 'I suppose you think she's cute?'

Yes. 'Is that the problem? You're jealous?'

'Of her?' Melanie said with a harsh screech in her laugh.

He felt the oddest desire to put his hands around her neck and squeeze.

'You're the one who asked if I thought she was cute.'

'Do you?'

He shrugged. 'You're not the only beautiful woman in the world, Melanie. You'd better hope I like you for more than that.'

'Do you?' she challenged.

He stared at her for a long time. He was uncomfortably aware that he couldn't answer her.

She drew in her breath sharply and turned from him. She walked away with a sway that showed off her every asset to best advantage. But she didn't seem as beautiful to him as she had when she had first got out of the car.

She got back in it, revved the engine unnecessarily, and left, squealing her tyres and leaving dark black rubber smudges on the pavement.

All he could think was that she was wrecking tyres he'd paid for.

He walked back up the hill. 'What are you looking at?' he snapped at Moose who was regarding him with a wry grin.

'Just thinking you'd probably have a bill for flowers tomorrow, huh, boss?'

'Yeah,' he said wearily. 'Between flowers and sky-hooks I'm going to wind up a poor man. OK, is this wall ready to go?'

He was ready for the wall. Pitting his strength against it would make him feel good. Back in control.

It was a big wall. He put Janey on one end of it, and Tuffy on the other. He and Moose took the middle of it where the weight was most concentrated. He was next to Janey. They crouched, knees bent, ready.

'Lift,' he shouted.

The wall groaned up a few inches. It was impossibly heavy. Four pairs of hands walked it slowly up, higher and higher. Janey could feel herself straining, giving everything she had. And for a frightening second she thought that wasn't going to be enough. The wall was going to fall back down on them.

Out of the corner of her eye, she could see Blaze's arm, stretched, bracing the wall, the muscle corded and gleaming in the bright afternoon sun. Suddenly she knew the wall wouldn't come back down because he wouldn't let it.

She could tell the moment the adrenalin hit him. It was as if he shifted from the defensive to the offensive.

The power rippled and surged down the length of his body. He let loose with a sound that was almost a war cry. The wall snapped up.

Her own arms remained braced, but she wiped her forehead on her sleeve, knowing she really just wanted to look at him, the male animal triumphant, his muscles still pumped from the test they had just passed, the cooling sweat curling down his face.

He looked happy. Contented. Sure in his strength and his manliness. This was his world.

And she suddenly didn't feel good that it was her most heartfelt desire to destroy it.

CHAPTER FIVE

'IT DON'T look like the flowers helped much,' Clarence muttered to Janey, as he set his lunch box down beside hers.

They had just arrived at work. It was a beautiful day, the morning sun burning a light haze off the landscape. She turned and pulled on her gloves, pretending to admire the view. Blaze was coming up the rise towards them, his stride long, his face set.

Clarence was right; it didn't look as if the flowers had helped much. Blaze looked like a man who had spent a most miserable evening.

She smiled nicely at him. 'Lovely day, isn't it?'

'If you think it's such a lovely day, why don't you pack yourself a lovely little lunch, take your lovely little self and have a lovely little picnic somewhere? And forget to come back.'

'You'd miss me,' she goaded him sweetly.

'Yeah. The same way you miss a sliver once it's been pulled out. Get to work. I want the outside walls done today.'

'Yessir, Mr Happy.'

'Geez, you're a lippy little thing.' He stamped by her, buckled his apron into place, shouted an order at Clarence, and went up the ladder.

A moment later she saw him walking casually along the top of a wall, graceful and sure-footed as an alley cat. A funny sensation tickled the back of her neck, and she suddenly wished he'd come down from there.

'Does he ever fall?' she asked Clarence, with a studied lack of concern.

'Sure. He went off the roof on our last job. Slipped in some sawdust. Boy, did he ever swear a blue streak then. You ain't never heard nothing like it in all your life.'

She was sure she hadn't.

She began sorting through the studs they would need for the next wall, cutting some of them down to 'cripples'.

She heard Blaze's startled cry, and whirled to see the wall he'd been walking on tilting crazily. His arms were windmilling, but there was nothing he could do to stop the wall.

In horror she watched as it fell inwards on to the floor, narrowly missing Tuffy. Blaze went off it the other direction. She was already running, and flew off the side of the house into a pile of dirt. He was lying on the other side of it.

She wished he'd swear, but he lay there looking at the sky, his mouth contorted with pain.

'Are you hurt?' She crouched beside him, swept his hair back from his brow, looked into his eyes. Oddly, her mind registered the fact that his hair felt like silk beneath her fingertips, and his eyes were two shades bluer than the sky.

'Yeah...hand. I...put out my...hand.'

She turned quickly to his hands. Her stomach somersaulted. A thick, rusty-looking nail had gone right through his palm, nailing his hand to a small piece of scrap wood.

'Pull it off, Janey,' he ordered.

She forced herself to stay calm, and think. 'No. You know better than that, Blaze. We'll have to get you to the hospital.'

'Lippy as ever,' he said, wincing against the pain.

'Clarence——'

She turned around. Moose had arrived and was towering behind her, his eyes fastened sickly on Blaze's hand. The colour was receding from his face.

'Moose, old buddy, pull this off of here, OK? The shrimp won't do it.' Blaze closed his eyes.

'Clarence!'

He fell as heavily as the wall had.

Blaze opened his eyes, looked at Clarence, shook his head and managed a weak grin. 'He can't handle the sight of blood. I guess I shouldn't have asked him to pull it off.' He grimaced, gathered himself, and then, with a groan, sat up. 'Look after Moose.'

There wasn't much she could do for Clarence, except turn him over so that he wasn't face down in the dirt. Tuffy was beside her suddenly, his face expressionless, as he helped her roll Clarence over.

'Now, can you help me get him——' she pointed to their other patient '—to my car?'

Tuffy nodded.

'That'll be the day I need help,' Blaze said. 'I can walk.' He got unsteadily to his feet, but didn't protest at all when she shoved herself under one of his arms and Tuffy did the same on the other side.

'We can take the truck,' he said when they got him down the hill. 'No sense using your gas on company business.'

She stared at him incredulously. 'At a time like this, you're going to think about business? Honestly, I don't think there's any hope for you.'

'I wasn't thinking about business,' he snapped back, the pain taking much of his usual vigour from his voice. 'I was thinking of *you*.'

'Me?' She was taken aback by that.

'You don't have to use your car for——'.

'Blaze, just shut up and get in the car before you bleed to death.'

'I'm hardly bleeding at all,' he pointed out querulously, but he went and got in her car without further protest.

He began to curse as soon as he was settled in the car.

'Hurts, huh?' she said, reaching across him to do up his seatbelt.

'Nah.' He said six words in a row she had never heard before. 'It doesn't hurt a bit.'

'Tuffy, could you get a cold cloth and put it on Clarence's forehead? When he comes to, put his head between his legs until he's more steady.'

Tuffy nodded.

'And don't let him moan and groan too long,' Blaze called. 'I want the outside walls up and——'

'Shut up, Blaze,' she ordered, getting in the driver's side, starting the engine and putting her foot to the floor.

'Cheeky woman.' He closed his eyes. 'Can't you drive any faster than that?'

'I thought you said it didn't hurt.'

'I lied. It hurts a little.' He groaned. 'And it seems to hurt a little more with each passing second.'

She glanced at him. He was pale and sweat was beading on his face.

'I can't believe that wall came down.' Another trail of very imaginative expletives followed that observation. 'This house is cursed. It's probably unlucky to have a woman on a job.'

'That's certainly a scientific explanation for what happened.'

'Biology is a science,' he said grimly.

'What does that mean?'

'Too many hormones hopping around. Clarence was supposed to anchor that wall. Ow! Slower on the bumps, Janey, you have an injured man here.'

'I can't go both fast and slow. And I can't believe you're going to try and blame me, indirectly, for what happened to the wall. I had nothing to do with it.'

'I didn't blame you, I blamed biology.'

'The Hopping Hormone Theory of Wall Collapse. Or is it a hypothesis until you prove it correct?'

'Janey, please don't make me laugh. It makes my hand wobble.'

'Then behave yourself, or I'll start telling dirty jokes.'

'Aw, Janey, I'd risk the pain to hear a dirty joke come off those prissy lips of yours.'

'I am not prissy!' she said with indignation.

'Sure you are. Everybody else works with their shirts off.'

'Forget it, Blaze.'

'Can't fault a man for trying. I bet you don't even know any dirty jokes.'

'I do so.'

'Then tell me one to distract me before I try to chew my hand off at the wrist.'

'I can't remember one at the moment.'

'Right.'

She was relieved to see the hospital just down the hill and to the right. She pulled in and brought the car to a halt in the section reserved for emergency vehicles. 'We're here.'

'And about bloody time, too. I've driven to the Sunday school picnic faster.'

'You've never been to a Sunday-school picnic in your whole life.' She got out of the car and dashed round to his side, unbuckled his seatbelt for him.

They went in and looked after the administration details. A doctor came and did a brief inspection of Blaze's hand.

'Air nailer, eh?'

'No, I fell on it.'

'OK, come with me.'

Janey sank down on to an ugly green vinyl couch. She looked at a rather vivid picture of an ulcer.

Her father was three floors away. She wondered if she had time to pop up and say hello to him. He and Blaze under the same roof, and she had just helped Blaze. Tuffy could have brought him here. She could have driven slower.

She didn't seem to be interested in causing him pain. Not physical. Not any other kind either. She decided it would be a bad idea to go and see her father right now.

The minutes ticked by. She flipped through an eleven-year-old magazine.

'Janey!'

She looked up, startled.

'Jonathan!'

'What are you doing here?' they asked together.

'I had a dental emergency come in. I was on call today.'

'My boss got hurt.'

She stood up, and couldn't help but notice that Jonathan hesitated before giving her the briefest of hugs.

She realised that even though she hadn't been working for very long when the accident happened there was sawdust clinging to her clothes. She realised he probably didn't want to be seen hugging a scruffy little carpenter's helper.

They made uncomfortable small talk for a few minutes, and then Blaze came out, his hand neatly wrapped in white gauze, a funny smile on his face.

'I gave him a pretty potent painkiller,' the doctor told Janey. He passed her a vial. 'He needs to take these. He won't be any good at work for a couple of days.'

The doctor disappeared.

'Jonathan, this is my boss Blaze Hamilton, Blaze, my fiancé Dr Jonathan Peters.'

Blaze offered his left hand, since his right was bandaged. She noticed that Jonathan winced slightly when Blaze shook his hand. She noticed that Blaze towered over Jonathan. She noticed that Blaze was the most beautiful shade of gold. She noticed that Blaze was about two axe handles wide at the shoulders.

She threw herself into Jonathan's arms and kissed him with vigour. She drew away from him and turned crisply to Blaze.

'I'll drive you home, Blaze.'

'Home? Hell, I'm going back to work.'

'The doctor said——'

'Ha. I could break that doctor in two like a pencil.' He regarded Jonathan thoughtfully. She hoped he wasn't going to say, This one too.

'None the less, you're going home.'

'Have you noticed she's cheeky?' Blaze asked Jonathan solemnly.

'Er—I can't say that I've noticed that.'

'Pretty bloody hard to miss.'

It was then she noticed that he was slurring faintly, swaying just a bit, like a big tree in a small wind.

'What do you think of when you look at her mouth?' Blaze demanded.

'Pardon?' Jonathan asked.

'Well, like do you think about her teeth, or what?'

'Janey has lovely teeth.'

'Lovely teeth,' Blaze echoed. 'Lovely teeth to take on her lovely picnic.'

'What picnic?' Jonathan asked.

'Jonathan, he's out of his head. The doctor must have given him some morphine.'

'The Sunday-School picnic,' Blaze informed Jonathan. 'Janey on a blanket, in a field of buttercups. Did you ever think about that?'

'I can't say I have,' Jonathan said a trifle wildly. 'I really must get back to the office. Good meeting you, Mr Hamilton. Janey, I'll see you tonight.'

'Bye, Jonathan.'

Somehow she managed to get Blaze back out to the car. She reached across him to do up his seatbelt, and he buried his nose in her hair.

'Buttercups,' he said softly. 'You make a man think of buttercups.'

'Blaze, stop it.'

'And picnics.' His lips grazed her cheek, and she jumped back so fast that she hit her head on the door-frame.

She went round to the driver's side and took a deep breath. She opened the door. 'Where do you live?'

'Your place or mine, baby?' he asked thickly.

'Yours,' she said tersely, 'and don't call me baby.'

''K, buttercup.'

'Don't call me that, either.'

'Janey is a buttercup,' he sang.

'What did they give you, for crying out loud?'

'Something to make the hurting stop, Janey-is-a-buttercup.'

'I take it it's working,' she said drily.

'I feel so happy.'

'Well, that's a change.'

'Janey is a buttercup,' he sang, 'and I'm a mean old bee.'

'Blaze, tell me where you live.'

He told her. On the way he serenaded her, off-key, about tiny people and tiny cars. He kept reaching over and accompanying himself on her car horn as he sang the chorus.

This car did seem too tiny for such a big man. He was too close to her. His shoulder kept brushing hers. He smelled strongly of soap and sunshine mingled.

Between all that—his slurred instructions, and his beeping her horn at random—she missed the turn to his place three times.

Finally, she pulled up in front of a luxury apartment condominium. She had never been so happy to be out of a car in her whole life. Hurriedly, she went around and opened his door.

'Undo your seatbelt,' she ordered, not wanting to lean across him again. Her skin still tingled where his lips had touched it last time.

'Can't. Hand hurts.'

'Your hand could be on fire right now, and you wouldn't feel a thing.'

'Skinny little doctor, could break him in two like a pencil,' he muttered thickly.

She was pretty darn sure he wasn't talking about the man who had worked on his hand.

'Good. With that kind of strength you should have no problem managing a little seatbelt.'

He finally figured out the intricacies of the seatbelt and tumbled from the car. She made him find his own crooked way up the straight path to the front door.

'Are you coming in, Janey-is-a-buttercup?'

She knew she shouldn't. She knew her duty was done. She'd had quite enough one-on-one exposure to Mr Blaze Hamilton for today. But she was this close, and she couldn't resist just a little peek into his lifestyle.

'I'll see you safely in,' she said with stiff propriety.

He began to hum a few bars of a song she knew to be about little Red Riding Hood and a big bad wolf.

She trailed him cautiously through the building to his ground-floor apartment. 'Did you build this place?' she asked, when it sounded as if he was going to start humming that song, for the third time, more loudly than he had hummed it the first two times—which had been plenty loud.

'Are you kidding? Look at the mess they made of the drywall. Wouldn't happen on one of my buildings.'

She studied the drywall, which was far safer than studying him. She could see a few tape marks.

He was struggling with his keys. 'I'm not building a place for me until——'

The door swung open abruptly and he fell in behind it. Regaining himself, he held the door open to her with a dignified bow.

'Until?' she prodded, moving by him. His place was very plain. A bachelor's home. No frills, no soft touches. There were two ultra-modern paintings on the wall above a sofa that looked as if it had come from a garage sale. She suspected he hadn't bought the paintings himself.

He had come and planted himself in front of her.

'Until I get married and have some kids. Houses aren't about places to live, they're about dreams. Kids laughing. Cookies baking. A fire in the hearth.'

'That's what you dream about?' she asked him with soft surprise.

He leaned very close to her. His eyes were half-lidded, and smoky. His voice was husky. 'There's more. The kids asleep, and the house quiet. A big brass bed, and a woman waiting, with a tender light in her eyes and the softest of smiles on her lips.'

A strangled kind of sound came from her throat.

He smiled wickedly, showing the strong line of those incredibly white teeth. 'They're just dreams, Janey. Nothing to be afraid of. Part of growing up is knowing the difference between a dream and reality.'

It made her feel faintly sad that Blaze didn't believe in his dreams, had let them go somewhere along the way.

'I think I gotta go to sleep, Janey-is-a-buttercup.' He smiled at her, a smile so sleepy and sensuous that it tied a knot in the bottom of her stomach that might never come undone. 'Want to come with me?'

'You don't even know what you're saying,' she said lightly, so lightly that he would never know how her heart was thudding in her throat.

'You got that right,' he admitted, and then, giving her a wave, wandered down the hall, and disappeared into a bedroom.

Now she should go. There was absolutely no further excuse for staying.

She heard the far-off creak and thud of him hitting the bed. She went to his fridge and opened it. She smiled. Two cans of Coke and a half-eaten can of sardines. No wonder Blaze was grumpy sometimes!

She unabashedly snooped through his cupboards. They were nearly as empty as the fridge. She saw a loaf of bread, a can of peanut butter, a jar of decaffeinated instant coffee, and three cans of tuna. On closer inspection, she also found some lemonade crystals.

She made a big pitcher of lemonade and some tuna sandwiches. She wrapped the sandwiches and put plenty of ice in the lemonade pitcher. He might wake up thirsty from the drugs. And she knew he'd wake up hungry. The man ate like a horse and it was almost lunchtime.

She put the items on a tray and carried them down to the bedroom.

And it was only once she was inside that she couldn't fool herself any more. The sandwiches and drinks were just an excuse. She had wanted to see his bedroom...and yes, she had wanted to see him, just like this.

He was sprawled on his stomach, crossways, on the bed, which was not brass, to her immense relief. He had managed to get his shirt off, and one boot.

She tiptoed in, half-afraid he might wake up and think he was going to have his picnic after all. She set down the tray on the table beside his bed.

The furniture in here was ordinary, picked for function rather than to create any kind of mood. The room had that same lack of personality his living-room had had. No pictures on the walls, no nice decorations, no handmade quilt or valance above the window.

Why did that make her feel the oddest twinge of tenderness for the big man breathing so deeply on the bed? Because he had shared with her a dream that was cosy and home-like, and the way he lived was so far from it?

She tugged off his other boot, and pulled the blanket up over him. Almost over him. For a minute, she could not bring herself to cover the golden curve of his shoulders. She looked at them. She hesitated. She touched his skin, and let her hand linger on that warm and silky surface for far longer than she should have.

Finally, with an odd reluctance, she pulled the quilt up over him, and looked at his sleeping face, marvelled at the fact that his lashes were so dark when he was so fair.

She longed to touch his cheek. She made herself turn and walk out of the room.

'How are you feeling?' she asked Clarence when she got back.

'I'm OK.' He looked shamefaced.

'You don't have to be embarrassed about fainting. That happens to many people.'

'It does? I mean, even to big guys like me?'

'Sure. Size doesn't have anything to do with it. I donate blood and I've seen all kinds of big guys faint dead away.'

'Really?' he said gleefully.

'Really,' she assured him.

'How's Blaze?'

'Drugged up pretty good on painkillers. He isn't supposed to work for a few days.'

'That won't stop him.'

'I guessed as much. I think the doctor did, too. That must be why he gave him enough drugs to take out a rhinoceros. I think he figured he'd keep him away at least for today. By the way, did you figure out what happened to the wall?'

'I don't like it. Somebody fooled with that wall.'

'What?'

Clarence led her over to the wall. 'Those look like crowbar marks to me.'

'Crowbar marks?'

'Where the braces were. I think somebody pulled the braces off then left them propped up to look as if they were still nailed together. As soon as Blaze put his weight on that wall—kapooey.'

'But why would anybody do such a thing?'

Another incident that didn't make sense to add to her list of incidents that didn't make sense. If anything, this latest accident pointed away from Blaze having any involvement in it. He wouldn't be up strolling along a wall he knew wasn't properly braced.

Plus, thus far, the incidents had been relatively minor. He hadn't had anything big enough happen to make an insurance claim. If anything he was probably losing money—and time—on the annoying little accidents.

Of course, he was a smart man. She could not help being impressed with his keen intelligence. He knew at a glance at the plans what would work and what wouldn't. He'd known immediately that the stairs were out on this plan. He used maths easily and often, figuring out angles and weight loads. He had organised the plan of the attack on the house with incredible efficiency, knowing exactly what order to do things in to make the most of his time and manpower.

If a man like that was sabotaging his own house, he would know how to make it look as if he wasn't. As if it was inconceivable that he was doing it.

Still, the bottom line was that as she got to know Blaze better it seemed more ludicrous, rather than more likely, that he would do anything underhanded. But then her feelings towards him were becoming more and more muddled. She had to think clearly; she had to remember what she had come here for.

For now, she would have to be satisfied with collecting pieces of a puzzle. For now, she would have to keep reminding herself that he *seemed* like many things, but he was still the man responsible for the fact that her father was in that hospital bed today.

She sighed. 'Tuffy, what do you think happened to the wall?'

He started and stared at her. She nearly backed away from the hostility she saw in his eyes. Nearly. Because just before she did she saw something else: fear. The kind of snarling fear of an animal afraid of being trapped.

He shrugged and turned away from her.

Did Tuffy know something about that wall that the rest of them didn't?

She sighed. 'Let's see if we can get the wall back up.'

Clarence and Tuffy had got several of the other walls up, but this one still lay there.

'It took all four of us before,' Clarence offered reluctantly.

'We can do it,' she said with determination.

Both Tuffy and Clarence turned and looked at her in amazement.

'I know,' she said cheerfully. 'I'm cheeky. And lippy. And bossy, too. But I think we can do this.'

But somehow she wasn't fooling herself. It wasn't because she was bossy that she wanted that wall back up. It was because some part of herself, some renegade part of herself was out of step with all the other parts of herself, and that one renegade part had this bizarre desire to make Blaze happy.

'Turn the wretched thing off,' Jonathan said grumpily.

Janey reached for the VCR remote control and turned off the film Jonathan had brought over.

'Do you want some more tea? Or popcorn?'

'I still have lots of tea.' He took a sip.

She knew something was on his mind. He could usually sit through the most wretched films quite blissfully. She waited.

'You never told me your boss looked like that,' he ventured conversationally.

'Looked like what?' she asked warily.

'Come on, Janey. If you stuck a surfboard under his arm he'd look those ads they use to lure people to California. You know that look—sun-streaked, muscular. Even his teeth looked absolutely perfect.'

'Oh. Didn't I ever mention he was kind of good-looking?'

'You know darn well you didn't. I was under the impression he was old and pot-bellied. I somehow pictured him smoking a cigar and yelling.'

'One out of four,' she said, with an attempt at humour. 'He yells rather well.'

'I just don't understand why you would keep it from me.'

Fight time, she thought wearily. 'I didn't think it would interest you what my boss looked like. Nothing else about my job seems to interest you.'

'Your quitting day interests me,' he muttered. 'Especially now.'

'Why "especially now"?'

'I didn't like that man. I don't like you working for him.'

For some reason she felt the oddest need to defend Blaze. 'What didn't you like about him, precisely?'

'I just dislike those macho types.'

'Were you threatened by Blaze?' she asked, though she wouldn't have really blamed him if he was.

Skinny little doctor, I could break him in two like a pencil.

'Threatened by that?' Jonathan squeaked. 'You must be joking. I know that kind. Probably has a fridge full of beer and holds belching contests with his friends.'

She had the oddest longing to throttle Jonathan. 'Oh. So men who work physically are crude and vulgar, are they?'

She decided against revealing that she knew, personally, that there was no beer in Blaze's fridge.

'I suppose so.'

'My dad was a building contractor,' she reminded him tightly. At one time tonight she had debated telling him the role her dad played in her going to work for Blaze Hamilton, but she had somehow changed her mind.

'Janey, I'm sorry. Don't be so sensitive. I guess maybe I was a little threatened by him. You don't find him attractive, do you?'

Yes. 'Jonathan, there are lots of attractive men out there. You have to trust me a little more than that. I'm not the type that throws myself at the feet of every attractive man I see.'

She remembered touching Blaze's naked shoulder while he slept. She wondered, uneasily, if she deserved the trust she was asking Jonathan for.

CHAPTER SIX

'I THOUGHT the doctor told you to take a few days off,' Janey said quietly from behind Blaze.

She had arrived early. He was already there. He looked extraordinarily masculine in faded jeans and a black cotton T-shirt. His right hand was still wrapped in white gauze.

He snorted disdainfully. 'Doctors probably take a few days off for a hang nail.'

It would probably be taking it too personally to feel that was some sort of dig at Jonathan.

She noticed that his hair was damp, and realised he must be fresh out of the shower. She looked more carefully at his hand.

'Did you manage to rewrap your hand yourself after you showered?' Somehow she couldn't imagine him being that neat about it.

Too late, she realised he probably hadn't spent the night alone.

'I didn't unwrap it. I put it in a plastic bag to keep it from getting wet.'

No indication there that he hadn't spent the night alone. But what did she care?

'Did you find the painkillers? I left them on——'

'I found them.' He said this with stinging curtness.

'Did you take some?'

'Look, Florence, real men don't take drugs.'

She planted her hands on her hips. 'You needn't make it sound like I asked if you smoked some funny-smelling green weed before you came to work. I asked if you followed the doctor's orders.'

'No. I didn't.'

'Oh? And why is that?' She could not believe this was the same man who had seemed to find her hair irresistible, who had sung softly, 'Janey-is-a-buttercup.'

'I'm not good at taking orders, just giving them.' He said this with a flat lack of apology.

He found something in his tool-box very interesting. He started pawing through it, with his uninjured left hand, with a vengeance that threatened to break things.

'You need your wits about you on a job like this,' he continued. 'You don't want to do anything stupid.'

'Oh,' she said, loading that one syllable with understanding.

He turned and glared at her. 'Did I?'

'Blaze, the doctor gave you something pretty strong for the pain...'

'Answer the question. Did I act stupid? Did I say things I didn't mean? Did I——?' His eyes trailed uncomfortably to her lips, and suddenly he seemed to find that tool-box very engrossing again.

'No, you didn't,' she answered swiftly, addressing the last question only.

'Great,' he muttered. 'Have you seen my level? I want to check that wall. It looks like it came out of it not too bad.'

Janey reached into his tool kit and extracted the level from the mess he had made.

'Clarence thinks the braces might have been tampered with.'

'I might say that too if it had been my job to secure the braces and then they didn't hold.'

'I don't think he was trying to cover himself,' she said hotly. 'He's not like that.'

But she knew her heat was less in response to what he'd said about Clarence than to the way he was treating her—with curt indifference. For some silly reason she had hoped maybe yesterday they had got over some sort of hump in their relationship.

But given the reasons she was here that was a foolish thing to hope for. A dangerous notion to entertain, even briefly.

'What is it with you?' he asked. 'Do you have to champion the whole world? Do you have to be so bloody nice all the time? Lemonade and sandwiches. Geez.'

'A simple thank-you would have sufficed,' she said stiffly, wounded to the core. But the dangerous notion to like him had died a quick death within her.

'If you want thank-yous, Nurse Nightingale, go work in a hospital. We like 'em rough and tough out here. Big helps, too. This is no place for a soft-hearted pipsqueak.'

'Are you back on that?'

'For your information, I never got off that.'

'It's too bad you don't like drugs,' she snapped. 'They improved your temperament immensely. You were almost a pleasure to be around.'

Jerk, he called himself when she walked away. His hand felt as if it was on fire. He should have taken those pills, but dammit, he had a foggy memory of the way he had acted yesterday. He felt like an idiot. Janey-is-a-buttercup. He didn't want to let his defences down too far, and for some reason drugs always turned him to mush. Even a bottle of beer put a faint foggy feeling in his head that he hated, which explained why he hadn't had a drink in probably close to ten years.

Lout, he called himself. He should have thanked her for the sandwiches.

He'd woken up and found them, and that pitcher of still cold lemonade, and he been so damned grateful he'd thought he was going to bawl. It had been a long time since anyone had looked after him. Since he had allowed anyone to look after him. It made him feel...vulnerable.

That was a feeling he didn't much like. And he sure as hell didn't want her to know he'd felt it. She didn't even like him, for God's sake. She was going to marry a stupid little dentist whom he could break in two as easily as a pencil.

But who probably knew how to say 'thank you'. And 'I'm sorry'.

Not that he cared. Maybe he'd get married himself. Melanie had been hinting in that direction. And if he got married in December he'd get a hell of a tax break.

Melanie didn't want kids. And she didn't know how to bake cookies. But then he was old enough to know by now that dreams and reality were two entirely different things. Dreams were things you kept inside you, took out and looked at now and then in the privacy of your own head. It would be ruddy dangerous to start believing in the silly things.

It was having her around that was stirring these vague feelings of discontent in him. This vague longing for...what?

He saw her greet Moose with a big grin, and then hand him a little brown bag.

Moose looked inside and his smile could have swallowed his face. He took out a home-made chocolate-chip cookie and popped the whole thing in his mouth. He closed his eyes and he chewed with slow ecstasy.

If I weren't such a jerk, I might be eating chocolate-chip cookies right now.

'Runt, if you want to open a cookie shop—an admirable pursuit for one of the female persuasion—go do it,' he yelled. 'But if you want to work for me I better hear a hammer hitting wood in three seconds. I want these inside walls done *yesterday*.'

He stormed off the floor and went and looked at the wall that he had fallen from, from the outside.

He looked at the two-by-fours that were bracing it.

'Moose, are these the same braces we used yesterday?'

'Yup.'

Blaze frowned, and ran his hand thoughtfully over the scars in the wood where nails had been pulled. Was someone sabotaging his job? It seemed unlikely. For what reason? Just kids fooling around at night? Did they know the consequences of what they were doing? That they could get somebody killed?

His hand felt as if an elephant was practising standing on one leg on top of it.

Janey had everything under control inside. She was right. She was worth twelve dollars an hour—more if she was going to bring home-made cookies to work. Clarence was working like a man inspired.

With a stifled groan of pain, Blaze went and got in his truck and roared away.

* * *

'Yes, Mr Hamilton, the grant was approved. Just let me find the file.'

He looked round the employment office. This was the type of place where a woman should be working. Warm. Dry. Safe. Civilised. The heaviest thing she'd have to lift in a day would probably be a stapler.

Janey would hate it in here, he thought. Because I hate it in here.

'There seems to be a problem, sir.'

He held his temper. Why were there always problems whenever you dealt with the government?

'Our computer isn't accepting Miss Smith's——'

Ms, he corrected her mentally. Soon to be Mrs, he reminded himself sourly.

'—social insurance number. Maybe one of the digits is incorrect. Could you check it, and bring it back to us?'

'Yeah, sure.' He'd probably get his grant after Janey Smith was a distant memory of lemon-scented soap. He stuffed the papers in his pocket, and for the first time in his memory cast around for a reason not to go back to work.

The elephant was practising pirouettes on his hand now. He could go home, take a couple of those pills, and flake out for the afternoon.

But then yesterday, his drug-hazed dreams had been haunted by her. Maybe he should go back to work, and work on getting her to quit some more. At least that had been fun. If he couldn't get her out of his mind, at least he could take his mind off the searing pain in the palm of his hand.

'Blaze, boss, I gotta talk to you.'

It was lunchtime. Moose's breath was heavy with the

smell of chocolate-chip cookies. He had clenched Blaze's shoulder in a hard, hurting grasp.

'I did something real stupid.'

Blaze cast an anxious glance at his Skilsaw. It seemed to be in one piece. The cord looked fine.

He prised the big hand from his shoulder. 'Relax. It can't be that bad.' Don't yell, he instructed himself.

'Remember Janey told me about that friend of hers?'

'I remember.'

'Well, she gave me her number. It took me three days to screw up the nerve to call her, but I finally did it. I phoned her last night. I made a date for tonight.'

'Great.' He gave Moose a congratulatory clap on the shoulder, and felt his own relief that it wasn't something that was going to cost him time or money. 'By the way, good work on the walls. I——'

'Blaze, what do I do now?'

'What do you mean what do you do now?'

'I ain't never been on a date, Blaze.' There was panic in those eyes, and Moose hung his shaggy head.

'Never?' Blaze asked incredulously.

'Look at me, Blaze. What kind of girl wants to go out with a gorilla?'

He looked at the man who had worked for him for seven years. He didn't see a gorilla. Or even a moose, for that matter.

'So what do you need to know, Clarence?'

Clarence sat down hopelessly on a stack of plywood. 'Everything. What to do. What to wear. And what to say. Can I kiss her? Hold her hand?'

The eyes turned on his were plaintive. 'I don't even have any clothes. Just work stuff. You can wear that in the Oasis.' Clarence stood up abruptly. 'I'll just have to tell her no. I can't. I'll cancel. That would be best, right, Blaze?'

He suspected that a week ago he would have just said, 'Right,' and walked away from it. But suddenly it seemed to Blaze as if the blinkers had been removed from his eyes. He saw the deep and tormenting loneliness in Clarence's eyes. And the fear—that he wasn't good enough; that he wasn't the same as everyone else; that he could never have what other people had because he didn't fit the stereotype of what attractive was.

He knew suddenly why he and Clarence had worked together for seven years: because they liked each other. Somehow over the course of the years they had become friends without his even noticing it. He cared about Clarence.

He was stunned by the discovery.

'Tonight, eh? I guess we don't have much time. Come on. We'll go get you some new jeans and a nice shirt. Have you ever had your hair cut by a hairdresser?'

Clarence was looking at him incredulously.

'You mean right now? With all this work to do?'

'Look, don't let it ever get around that I said this, but occasionally something is more important than work. Janey's got things under control here, anyway.'

'She sure does. She knows lots, doesn't she?'

'Not bad for a runt,' Blaze muttered.

'You really think I need a haircut from a store? I usually just cut my own hair.'

A week ago, he would have said, 'It shows.' Today he just said, 'I think for a special occasion you could lay out the ten bucks.'

'I hope her friend makes cookies,' Clarence said happily.

Blaze winced.

It was nearly six when he got back to the job site. He thought he'd put in an hour or two before the light failed. Hammering left-handed should be a challenge.

Something about Clarence's excitement, his *hope*, had created an emptiness in Blaze he wanted to fill.

He stood and regarded the structure from the road. Not bad, he thought. Behind schedule a bit, but there wasn't much he could do about that.

And then he heard the sound of a single hammer, and sought its source. She was still there.

He walked slowly up the hill, and up the board ramp into the house where in another week there would be stairs. He looked around as he entered the house, pleased with what he saw, pleased with the progress that had been made in his absence. He realised he had never hired anyone who showed any initiative before. He wondered why. He supposed he didn't like giving up control. He supposed he'd been using this job to fill a lot of spaces in his life for a long time. The more *he* had to do, the better he felt.

He wasn't sure if he liked knowing that about himself.

'Half-pint,' he called, not wanting to startle her. He came up behind her. There was a piece of wood tangled in one of the curls at the back of her head. He resisted the impulse to remove it.

She glanced over her shoulder at him, then kept on working. The light was always so beautiful at this time of day, and it threaded its way through the skeleton of a house to illuminate her in the most astonishing shade of gold.

'Quitting-time has come and gone,' he said softly.

Janey was aware that she didn't want to look at him. The shade of light at this moment was exquisite, and it would do magic things to his already magnificent colouring.

'I kind of lost track of the time. I like this part of building a house.'

'Me, too. You can really see things starting to happen.'

'Where did Clarence go this afternoon?'

'Uh, he had some personal stuff he had to do.' The last thing he was going to admit to her, after his rough and tough speech this morning, was that he had just spent the afternoon coaching a frightened Clarence on how to survive an evening with a member of the opposite sex.

'Blaze, I made an awful mistake this afternoon.' She slid her hammer into her apron, took a deep breath and turned to face him. Her heart was beating in her throat.

His eyes flew to his Skilsaw.

'Do I finally get to fire you?' he asked hopefully.

'I don't think you'll want to fire me. You're already a man short.' She took a deep breath and continued. 'When the wall came down yesterday I tried to ask Tuffy some questions about it. He wouldn't say anything.'

'He never says anything. That's just the way he is.'

'I thought maybe he was hiding something.'

'Tuffy? No. He's quiet. Maybe he's even hard. But he wouldn't ever hurt anybody, and he's honest as the day is long. I made a mistake on his cheque once—a couple of bucks in his favour. He brought back the money the next day.'

Sometimes Blaze seemed so insensitive, she thought, and yet he was far more sensitive to Tuffy than she had been. Maybe he had been right all along. Maybe a woman didn't belong in this world. She spoke a different language from these guys. Tuffy and Blaze communicated without even speaking, for heaven's sake.

'I tried to get him to talk about it again today. When he wouldn't talk I kind of got stubborn——'

'You, stubborn?' he interjected with a disbelieving look.

'And I pushed at him——'

'Physically?'

'Of course not.'

'No, of course not. With a tongue like yours, you don't need muscle.'

'Blaze, he left!'

'You tormented the poor man till he walked off the job?'

'Exactly,' she said sadly.

Blaze started to laugh. 'I must say I can sympathise with him. Here I thought the man was the only sane one here.' He could have said the only one here immune to you, but he didn't.

'Aren't you angry?'

'No.'

'Why not?'

'Would you like me to be?'

'I'd feel more comfortable if you were angry, instead of standing there looking at me as if you find me faintly amusing.'

'You are kind of cute when you're admitting you're wrong.'

'That's better,' she said drily. 'At least it's sexist. Aren't you the least bit worried about being a man short for a while?'

'He'll probably be back. Tempers fly on jobs like this, Janey. I wouldn't worry about it.'

'What if he doesn't come back?'

'I'll drop around and see him if he doesn't come in tomorrow.'

And tell him not to let the woman get under his skin, she guessed.

'Why don't you go home now that you've had your confession?'

'Thank you, Father Hamilton,' she said drily, 'but if you don't mind I'll just stay a while longer. I'd like these inside walls finished today, too.'

'I don't pay overtime.'

She shrugged. 'It doesn't matter.'

Shoot. The man of his dreams was a woman! 'And you don't have to atone for your sins.'

'I like it.'

'You like it?' he asked softly.

'I like working. I like being outside at this time of day.'

'Me, too.'

Side by side, in comfortable silence, they finished the inside walls. They were working in the dark by the time the last nail went in.

'Come on, let's go grab a hamburger.'

'You mean together?' she asked.

'Sure. I'll even buy.'

'Getting a lot accomplished does as much for your temperament as a double dose of painkiller,' she commented.

'Yeah,' he said gruffly. 'Remember that.'

'How does your hand feel?'

'I'll live.'

'Does it hurt?'

'Hell, yes, it hurts. Not enough to keep me from eating three double Joe burgers, though. And fries. Get in the truck.'

'Why don't men like to admit when they're in pain?' She got in the truck.

'And a double-thick shake.'

'You haven't answered my question.'

'Because women aren't attracted to men who are rolling on the floor crying that they have a pain.'

'That's silly.'

'It's the truth.'

'Men are motivated in their behaviour by what they think women want?'

'Look, runt, you're twisting my words. Making everything complicated. Men act like men. I don't know why. I sure don't want to spoil my enjoyment of a Joe burger trying to figure it out.'

She had never been to Joe's before. It was an old-fashioned burger joint with no frills and the best tasting hamburgers she had ever eaten.

'Not exactly heart smart, is it?' she said, digging into her hamburger and fries.

'If you're going to worry about that, go sit in the truck.'

'I wasn't worried, precisely. I just——'

'Look, the last time I had a physical, the doctor told me I was in better shape than two professional athletes who were also his patients, and that I could run any man ten years younger than me right into the ground.

'Our bodies are made to work. They crave it. All these people go for aerobics workouts, but I get my workout at work and I don't pay anybody a thousand bucks a year for the privilege of being in shape.

'And I eat hamburgers any time I feel like it.'

'There's no need to turn a simple comment into World War Three.'

He grinned 'You're right. There isn't. What's safe ground for us? Tell me about you. Tell me how you know so much about building houses.'

This might be safe ground for him, but she was aware of entering a minefield.

'My dad was a contractor.'

'Really? From around here? I probably know him.'

'Not from around here,' she lied hastily. 'Back East. Anyway, I had three brothers, and I became a tomboy. My brothers always worked for my dad on holidays and in the summers, and I always did, too. My dad didn't like it much at first——'

'Something like me,' Blaze noted.

'—but I liked it. I could make better money doing that than doing girl jobs like babysitting or being a carhop, and I loved it. I liked being outside. I liked the very things you were just talking about—my body feeling so strong, and healthy from all that hard work.'

'Where are you from back East?'

Her hamburger was beginning to lose its taste. That was where lies got you—into more and more lies. 'Toronto,' she blurted out, though the closest she'd been to Toronto was a postcard a friend had sent her.

'Really? What part of Toronto?'

She took a mighty bite of her hamburger, so that she could think while she chewed.

'Wildwood,' she blurted out. She had no idea if there was a Wildwood in Toronto, and she hoped he didn't either. The bad taste was growing in her mouth. She didn't tell lies. She had always prided herself on being so honest.

'What about you, Blaze? How did you get into this business?'

'I wanted to make money,' he said simply.

Her heart sank. Money. Was he a man who would do anything for money, after all, even though that was not how he seemed? But didn't she already know that? Hadn't she come into this forearmed with that knowledge?

'I also can't stand being inside. I'm like a caged tiger. Can you picture me behind a desk?'

'No,' she admitted, 'I can't.'

He sighed. 'Melanie can. She thinks I should just handle the administrative end and subcontract all the work. I could do more houses that way.'

'So, I guess there's more to it than making money, after all,' she noted with a satisfaction she didn't really understand.

He gave her a crooked smile. 'Don't let that get around. But yeah, I guess maybe there is. I have all this energy. I've never been able to sit still. It gives me a kind of satisfaction that I've turned the very thing teachers always yelled at me for into a way to make my living.'

She laughed. 'And a better living than most of them make.'

'I do OK. I don't seem to have much interest in being a high roller. Which drives——' His eyes suddenly went to the clock. 'Oh, hell. I forgot I was supposed to meet Melanie for dinner tonight.'

She dropped her own hamburger. 'Oh, no!'

'You too, eh?' he said wryly.

'I was supposed to meet Jonathan at Timber's——'
her own eyes drifted to the clock '—eight minutes ago.'

'I could get you there in five.'

'I can't go dressed like this.'

'Timber's. Right. A little more swanky than this,' he
said. There was a hood over those blue eyes as he looked
at her. 'I was going to bring Melanie here. She just hates
it.'

'Why would you bring her to a place she hates?'

'I keep trying to get her to like me just the way I am.'

'But don't you have to extend the same courtesy to
her?' Why was she defending Melanie? So far, she didn't
like much she'd heard about Blaze's girlfriend.

She decided not to wait for his answer. She didn't want
to know anything about his relationship.

'Excuse me, I have to go use the phone.'

She called Jonathan. He was understandably furious.
She offered to meet him later for a drink. He refused.

'You could always send him flowers,' Blaze suggested
when they were back in the truck, heading back to the
construction site for her car.

She looked at him. He seemed inordinately pleased
that Jonathan was mad at her, and not at all intimidated
by the fact that he had missed his own date.

'What did Melanie say?'

'She said I was a selfish, self-centred son-of-a-bitch,
and she hoped I choked on the hamburger. She said it
nineteen different ways and in six languages.'

Janey burst out laughing. 'Does that bother you?'

'It's mostly true. I'm not great at the finer things, like
being thoughtful.'

'I don't think that's true,' she said. She ordered herself
to shut up. It *had* to be true. That was why she was here.

But her voice ignored her order. 'I think maybe you just haven't met the person you want to be thoughtful for. I don't think love is a big job that you have to work at all the time—I think it's a pleasure that you just have to be open to.'

'Is that how you feel about Jonathan?' he asked gruffly.

She was stunned by the question. Even more stunned by the definition that had come so spontaneously from her lips.

'Yes,' she finally blurted out because the silence had become like an indictment.

But she knew it was just another lie in this night of so many of them.

But when had she started lying to herself?

'Oh, before I forget——' he pulled some very crushed papers from his shirt pocket '—is this your social insurance number?'

She squinted through the darkness at it. 'Yes.'

'Idiots at that office. They said the computer keeps spitting it out.'

But not because of her social insurance number, she thought unhappily, because of another lie. Her last name was not Smith.

She went and visited her dad that night. He seemed worse, hanging on to life by some fragile thread.

She went home and fell asleep on her couch watching some ridiculously romantic film from the forties. She woke up with tears on her cheeks. She had been dreaming, the dream accurate in every detail of that night eight years ago.

She had been sixteen again. They had been eating dinner. Dinner was always so laughter-filled as her brothers and her dad exchanged taunts, and teased her and her mother until they were squealing in protest.

The doorbell had rung.

'I'll get it,' Janey had sung.

She'd gone and opened the door.

He was standing there, as big as a mountain. Blond and as gorgeous a man as she had ever seen. Her teenaged heart had done back-flips. She'd smiled at him, and even practised a little inexpert flick of her eyelids.

But he hadn't seemed to notice, something grim in his eyes, and in the hard set of his mouth. 'I need to talk to Sam Sandstone. Now.'

She had been startled. Nobody walked into Sam Sandstone's house and started giving orders.

She had let him in, gone and got her father, stood in the background watching as her father went to the door, and greeted the man.

'Blaze! This is a surprise! Something wrong on the job?'

'Yes, sir. Something's wrong on the job.'

What had been in Blaze Hamilton's eyes at that moment? Killing contempt? For the father she worshipped. She had started to hate Blaze Hamilton right then.

She had seen her father, who had never faltered, falter.

'Come into my office, son. We'll talk about it.'

She couldn't very well listen, but after a while the voices had begun to rise. Or her father's had. Her father had bawled like a wounded bull. And the other man's voice had been cold, insistent—lethal, she remembered thinking.

Blaze Hamilton had left a few minutes later, his face set in remote, ruthless lines.

She didn't know the exact words that had been spoken in her father's office that night. She only knew that they had never laughed around the dinner-table again. She only knew that the family fortunes had gone into a decline that was both rapid and stunning, and so had her father's health. He'd looked worried and tired, and he'd muttered under his breath about Blaze Hamilton having ruined him, ruined all his dreams for his family. Several days after that meeting he'd had the first of a series of heart attacks that would plague him for the next eight years.

Janey never asked him the specifics of that night. In her heart, she felt she *knew*. That horrible man had blackmailed her wonderful father, who, proud until the end, had never shared the details with her.

Somehow in her mind she believed that if only she could salvage some of the dignity her father had lost that night so long ago there would be hope for him. And maybe he could salvage some of that dignity if she did what he had not done—brought Blaze to justice, gave him a taste of the humiliation of failure. But she would have to catch him at his game. And she was no closer to doing that than the day she had started working for him.

She was not even any closer to knowing what his game was.

'Blaze, you were wrong about the movie.'

'Wrong about the movie?' Blaze asked Clarence absently.

'You said we might not have nuthin' to talk about, so take her to a movie, but we had lots to talk about. Lots. We didn't go anywhere near the movie house.'

But Blaze wasn't listening to Clarence, he was looking at Janey. He noticed how puffy her eyes were. He'd been around long enough to know what a woman who had spent the night crying looked like.

Dr Dentist must have given her a really hard time about missing their stupid date. That little weasel needed a talking to.

Sure, Blaze, he told himself. By you? The expert on romance who came home last night to find a chopped-up pink dress in front of your door?

It might have been smart to tell a little lie when Melanie had asked if the rookie happened to be the one he'd worked late with. But he wasn't a man accustomed to lying. He had a feeling there weren't going to be any December weddings, after all.

'Are you going to see her again?' he asked Clarence.

'You bet. She's going to take me line-dancing on Saturday night.'

Blaze wasn't sure what line-dancing was, but he sure as hell knew that look in Clarence's eyes.

A week ago he might have given into the impulse to tell him to run for his life. Today, he kept oddly silent.

When had he started wanting to believe in happy endings?

CHAPTER SEVEN

'CLARENCE, you look wonderful,' Janey told the big man, trying to get beyond her own weariness, her crushing sense of being heartsick.

'Thank you. I got my hair cut at a beauty parlour. First time I've ever been in a parlour that didn't sell beer.' He laughed with gusto.

'How did everything go?'

'Mabel really liked me,' he informed her confidentially.

'And did you like her?' Janey asked with a smile.

'Oh, yes.'

She waited for Blaze to bellow at them to get to work. He was looking right at them but he didn't say a word.

'You don't look so hot today, Janey, or so happy.' Concern suddenly marred the shining happiness in Clarence's eyes.

'My dad's really sick right now, Clarence,' she was surprised to hear herself saying. 'Sometimes I just feel sad.'

'Aw, gosh, Janey, I'm sorry. What's wrong with him?'

'He's had heart problems for a number of years. He's in the hospital again.'

'That's rough, Janey.' The look in his eyes made it very apparent that his heart was the very same size as the rest of him. 'You let me know if I can do anything, OK?'

'Thank you.' She touched his arm in gratitude and he put his big hand over hers for a second before he returned to work. Her eyes drifted to Blaze. He was the only person who might be able to pull her father from that pit he had descended into. And he could only do it by going down himself.

'Did I tell you Blaze helped me pick out some nice duds for my date?' Clarence asked conversationally.

'Blaze did what?'

'He took me to a good store yesterday and we picked me up some nice jeans and a shirt for my date. I wanted a real nifty one that was blue and purple Paisley, but Blaze said maybe a guy my size should wear solid colours. I got a real nice navy blue one. It didn't have pearl buttons, but it was still real nice.'

'Blaze helped you get ready for the date?' She stared at Clarence incredulously. Blaze the Terrible?

'Yeah. I didn't even know what to say, so Blaze kind of coached me.'

'And how did he do that?' Janey asked, trying to sound only mildly interested.

'Oh, he told me to ask her lots of questions about herself and stuff.'

'Really?' 'Tell me about you,' Blaze had said to *her* over their hamburgers last night. Smooth as a snake, and just as sneaky, she warned herself.

Still, what kind of snake was it that gave someone else the kind of time and attention Blaze had given Clarence yesterday? A snake that was not rotten right through to the middle?

But hadn't that been her worst fear about Blaze for a long time? That a man could be good and bad both?

She didn't like that. She didn't like the confusion that was swirling like a prairie dust storm inside her.

Who was he?

She let her eyes drift to him again. A building inspector she recognised from a previous inspection was coming up the rise, and Blaze was going out to greet him. She watched him, fascinated, despite herself, by the way the sun danced on that fair hair, and highlighted the muscle ridges on his bare golden arms.

Her eyes narrowed. She couldn't believe what she was seeing. She wanted to turn away, but she couldn't. This was exactly what she had been waiting for. Why did she feel sick, instead of triumphant?

Why did the confusion inside her grow, instead of die out completely?

Blaze had his wallet out. Right there, in broad daylight, she watched him pass the building inspector a sheaf of bills. She was too far away to make out the denominations, but that part didn't really matter.

She turned to see if Clarence had seen, but he was completely engrossed in what he was doing. She turned back to her own work, but it felt as if she carried the weight of the whole world on her shoulders.

What next? What on earth did she do now?

'Morning, Blaze.'

'Hi, Cal. Better go over it with a fine-tooth comb today.' He and Cal had grown up in this area together. Though they had never actually been friends, there existed a mutual respect and liking between them.

'I was hardly going to look at it, Blaze. I know the quality of work you do.'

'I've had some vandalism of a fairly serious nature. I've been checking every morning for problems, but I'd hate to miss something.'

'What kind of vandalism problems?' Cal's dark brow lowered.

Blaze told him. Cal let out a concerned whistle. 'That's pretty serious stuff. Are you going to call the police?'

'If it happens again, I will. Who knows? Maybe it was just bad luck.'

'Maybe.' Cal's attention drifted towards the house, and then he grinned wickedly. 'I see the girl's still here.'

'Yeah.' For some reason he felt oddly offended every time someone called Janey a girl. It was as if they did not understand the full threat of this situation, the full weight of what he was dealing with. Couldn't any man with half an eye see that, despite her diminutive size, that was one full-blooded, red-hot woman up there working on his house?

'Pay up, then. You put ten bucks on having her out of here in a week.'

'Double or nothing?'

'Nah. She looks darn near finished now.'

Blaze felt a ripple of concern go through him. And anger. He'd like five minutes alone with Dr Dentist. He fished through his wallet and handed Cal a couple of ones and a five.

He was kind of glad Cal hadn't taken his bet. He would have lost again. It was one thing to go head-on with her when she was fighting fit. It would be quite another to pick on her today, when her eyes were big with some unspoken sadness, and there were tired little circles under her eyes, and there was the oddest little droop to the set of those usually feisty shoulders.

If you really wanted her to leave, you wouldn't hesitate to give her a good kick while she was down, a voice inside his head mocked him.

That wouldn't be very manly, he snapped back at it. He tried to dismiss her from his mind, but by coffee-break it hadn't worked.

He sidled over to Clarence. 'What's the matter with Janey today? She have a fight with the dentist?'

'She doesn't look like herself, does she?' Clarence sent her a look loaded with concern. 'She's says her dad's sick and it makes her sad.'

It wasn't until Blaze found out it had nothing to do with the boyfriend that he realised how badly he wanted her relationship to be in trouble.

The thought of her being sad about her father did a funny thing to his heart. He wanted to go over to her and wrap his arms around her, pull her into his chest and let her cry.

A funny feeling went through him. *Déjà vu*, some people would call it. A sense of having had this same feeling, this exact same feeling, in a different place and time.

He shook his head, trying to rid himself of the unwanted feeling. Nothing was the same, he thought unhappily, not since the moment she'd arrived.

And sometimes it felt as if nothing would ever be the same again.

Janey looked up to see Tuffy coming towards her. She was relieved to see him back, and also a little frightened. He'd looked angry when he left yesterday, and though he didn't look angry now he looked as remote as she had ever seen a man look.

He came and stood right in front of her, silently, his chilly blue eyes examining her face.

'Good morning,' she said nervously.

He reached into his shirt pocket and passed her a neatly folded note. What was it? A signed confession?

She noticed that the paper was light pink, and she bit back a nervous desire to laugh. She unfolded the note-paper, and looked at neat and very feminine handwriting.

'It is hard for Thomas to talk with people who aren't family. He has a speech impediment.'

Janey stared at the paper for a long time, sensing the love and the pride that had gone into this brief note, sensing the courage it had taken the man in front of her to ask someone to write it for him instead of walking away and never coming back.

She took a deep breath, and looked at Thomas. His expression was fierce and proud. But she did not see the chilliness in his eyes any more. She saw the small boy who had been taunted by children, and treated unkindly by teachers. She saw the young man who had been mocked by the tough men of these rough environments until he had chosen silence and a toughness of his own to hold the world at bay.

She burst into tears. She had never been so wrong about a person and she was so ashamed.

Thomas's expression changed from defensive to baffled and then to plain scared. He looked around for help, and when none was forthcoming he looked as if he would bolt. But he didn't. Something in those hard, guarded features softened, and after only another moment's hesitation he put his arms around her.

'Ere, ere,' he attempted to soothe. 'It kay. It kay.'

The severity of his speech impediment made her cry harder. His kindness made her cry harder. The poor man had been trapped so long in the prison of not being able to speak. He looked hard and wary so that the world would leave him alone, never find out. And nobody had seen through it. Certainly not her. And certainly not Blaze. How could he not have known this? she thought, feeling fresh anger at her employer.

'I'm sorry,' she sobbed. She felt so tired. So confused. All the mixed-up feelings seemed to be pouring out of her, and Thomas seemed to be prepared to hold her until she was finished.

'Let go of her. Right now.' The words were spoken softly. Too softly.

She looked over Thomas's shoulder, and saw that Blaze had come upon them.

Or you're a dead man, his flashing blue eyes said.

Thomas's arms dropped from around her, and he turned and faced Blaze. She darted in front of him.

'Blaze, no! It's not like that. Thomas wasn't hurting me.'

'*Thomas*,' he said flatly. 'OK, what was *Thomas* doing, then? And maybe *Thomas* should speak for himself.'

She saw the flash of pain in the wiry little man's eyes before the defences came up.

'Can I show him this?' she asked gently, holding up the little pink note. 'Please?'

Thomas shrugged as if it didn't make any difference to him.

'Look, Blaze.' She passed him the note. He took it and scanned it. The battle readiness faded completely from his features. The panther-coiled tension relaxed in his shoulders.

'I'm sorry, Thomas,' he said with such genuine humility that she thought she was going to start crying all over again. 'I didn't know. I only knew you and Janey had had some sort of disagreement yesterday. When I came around the corner and saw you holding her and her crying, I jumped to the wrong conclusion. I'm sorry.'

Thomas nodded with dignity, and with understanding. Janey knew, suddenly, that Thomas liked Blaze very much. Which only added to her confusion.

'I guess I misunderstood you when you told me your name the day you started here,' Blaze continued softly. 'You didn't say Tuffy, did you?'

Thomas shook his head.

'I'll remember to call you Thomas. If there's anything else I can do, let me know. The company medical would probably cover seeing a specialist, if you wanted to.'

Again that dignified nod, and then Thomas walked away.

'How could you not know?' Janey asked Blaze with soft accusation.

'Look, lady, at this precise moment in time I don't need you to tell me I'm an ass, OK? I happen to be well aware of the fact, and I'm not feeling very proud of it. I don't need a lecture from Miss Nightingale.'

'I am not——'

'And don't you start pressuring that man to see a specialist. If he wants help, he'll ask for it. If he had wanted anyone to know he had that speech impediment he would have told someone long before now. He only revealed it because his back was against the wall, not as an invitation for you to take over his life.'

'As if I would,' she spluttered indignantly. 'How dare you suggest I'm a do-gooder?'

'And by the way, since you're contending for this year's goodness-and-light award, how come you've never asked me my *real* name?'

'Your real name?' she echoed.

'Aw, never mind. I've got roof trusses coming, and I'm not ready. Just what I need to make a perfect day— a crane sitting here eating a hundred bucks an hour while I run sensitivity training.'

He turned and stomped away from her. Somewhere in the back of his mind it occurred to him that he'd started out to find her just to tell her he was sorry about her dad being sick.

That would teach him to try and be the New Male.

Besides, when he sneaked a glance back at her that little squabble seemed to have done her far more good than all his well-intended sympathy would have done. The colour was flying in her cheeks, and her eyes were spitting fire.

'That's more like it,' he muttered to himself.

Janey had taken exactly two bites from her sandwich when Blaze said three words in a combination she had never heard before. She could actually feel her ears turning red.

He had been eating and moving at the same time, when suddenly he'd glanced at the road and gone stock-still and said those three words. Then he'd actually slid her a look she could almost interpret as guilty before he'd looked back to the road with an exasperated sigh.

'What?' she asked him. She'd seen him lose his temper. She'd seen him put the full force of his will into getting a wall up, or getting Moose moving. But she had never seen him look... agitated.

'Owners,' he said, managing to load that one word with incredible pathos. 'What a day.'

She could tell he was about to follow that with a trail of words that would leave little doubt about his frustration with the day, but again he gave her that funny little look, and clamped his mouth shut instead.

'Is there something wrong with these owners?' she asked carefully.

'Not with these ones, with all of them.'

'I'm not following you.'

'Those people coming toward us with the starry expressions on their faces——' he squinted '—and the two babies stuck under their arms, are looking at their dream. Can you tell?'

She could tell, and she thought it was a wonderful thing to behold.

'They're also, most likely, spending more money than they've ever spent before.'

He said that as if she was supposed to draw some sort of conclusion, but she was as baffled as ever. 'And?'

'Dreams and bad nerves—lousy combination,' he muttered.

'Why?'

'It's usually starts with her: Gee, the kitchen isn't as big as I imagined it would be. Do you think you could move this wall? Could you put a skylight in the bathroom? Can this closet be moved over there? Could we do a bay window instead of a picture window? And then he'll start: Could we have a double garage instead of a single? What about finishing the basement?'

'Blaze——' she started laughing '—you're working yourself into a frenzy over nothing.'

'I am not in a frenzy,' he said with dignity. 'And it is not nothing. It's time and it's——'

'Money,' she guessed sourly.

'Look, it would be wonderful if we lived in a world where money didn't mean anything, but that's not for real. If you want to live like that, go be a missionary in Africa, or run a home for handicapped kids. But get off my construction site.'

'I know you don't mean that. You're just nervous.'

'I don't get nervous,' he snapped. 'But people want their bloody houses to make them *feel* things. They think this house is going to make them *feel* happy. Guess who bears the full brunt of it when they find out it ain't so? If they were unhappy before, they're still going to be unhappy, and a dozen skylights in the bathroom aren't going to fix it.'

'Well, they don't look unhappy. They look like nice people,' she said softly. She smiled. The dad was trying to carry two wriggling babies, maybe eighteen months old, under his arms like footballs. 'I'll show them around. Would that be OK?'

'OK?' Blaze breathed. 'OK? If you show them around I'll——'

'Never call me runt or pipsqueak again?'

'That's a hard bargain.'

'Hello, Blaze,' the young man said.

'Deal,' Blaze agreed desperately. 'Dave, Caroline, this is Janey Smith. She's going to show you around.' He looked at the babies and obviously felt some obligation to make small talk. 'Nice kids,' he said brusquely, and walked away.

Not a diplomat, Janey thought with a smile.

The young couple were staring at Janey with such astonishment that they had probably totally missed his lack of diplomacy.

'You're working on *our* house?' Dave finally asked, as if he harboured a sudden fear that the house might fall down around his ears while he slept.

'You needn't say it like that,' his wife reprimanded him.

'Can I take one of those?' Janey said, holding out her arms.

'Thanks. Caroline isn't supposed to carry them right now.' A pleased blush suffused his fair skin.

'Congratulations,' Janey said, accepting the baby. She tickled him under the chin and made him smile, and then planted him on her hip.

'I'm a carpenter's helper on this house. I like doing the job, and I'm good at it, too.'

'I wasn't suggesting you weren't,' Dave said apologetically, 'I was just a little surprised, that's all.'

'I happen to think it's simply wonderful,' Caroline said.

'Thank you. Blaze is trying to get ready for trusses, and the crane that brings them in costs quite a bit of money, so it would be better if I showed you around today. Do you know what trusses are?'

They both shook their heads.

'They used to use rafters to hold up the roof, but for the past, oh, twenty years, or maybe even twenty-five...' She told them about their trusses.

'Then we'll be ready for the roof. That will take about four days. Another day, or two, will be spent on windows and stairs, and then the framing is finished and the house is done to the stage called lock-up.'

'We might be able to move in sooner than we thought!' Caroline exclaimed happily.

'Probably not.' Janey smiled at her excitement. How could Blaze not like being a part of so many hopes and dreams? Janey was thoroughly enjoying this. 'The completion date Blaze gave you will be right on the money.

Now all the subtrades will start coming in to do the inside work. It takes a long time, longer than the framing.'

'Oh,' Caroline said, 'is this the kitchen?' Her voice was ripe with disappointment. 'It looks so small. Maybe we could move this wall——'

'It really isn't small at all,' Janey assured her. 'It's just hard to envisage what it will look like finished. Just a second, and I'll get you the blueprint, so you can see it in relation to the rest of the house.'

She got the blueprint and Caroline was reassured. Janey guided them from room to room, giving them details about the building that she thought they probably wouldn't be aware of but might find interesting.

'Blaze never tells us things like this,' Caroline said. 'I always get the feeling he's kind of racing us through the house as fast as he can, don't you, honey?'

Janey stifled a laugh.

'Sweetie,' her husband said, 'he has a reputation for being honest, and for bringing his houses in on time and on budget. That's what's really important.'

Janey's good humour died. She didn't know what Blaze was up to, but she knew what she had seen this morning.

Maybe that was why he had so much trouble with the people end of his business. Maybe it was hard to be face to face with people you were cheating in some way.

There were so many things that just didn't add up, that just didn't make any sense at all.

However, she tried hard not to let her troubled frame of mind dampen the enthusiasm of this lovely young couple. She calmly talked them out of several changes she could tell were complete nerves, and explained to them what several others would mean in terms of cost and time, though she left the final decisions to them.

Blaze watched her out of the corner of his eye, dangling that baby on her hip. Every now and then she would switch hips, but she seemed as natural with that baby as if she'd been toting them all her life. Somehow he would have liked it better if she were a failure at 'womanly' things, like baking cookies and blowing bubbles at babies.

The couple wandered around the house for a long time. Finally, they left.

'OK,' he shot from the hip. 'What do they want?'

'They want their house to be on time and on budget,' she told him. He was aware of the hard scrutiny in her eyes.

'Well, that's no problem as long as they didn't add a wing, skylights, a kitchen island, and marble fixtures.'

'They were such nice people,' she said serenely. But again there was a look in her eyes he didn't understand.

He stared at her. 'You just spent an hour with them, and you still like them?'

'It's a good thing you know how to build houses, Blaze, because your personality sure wouldn't sell you as a contractor.'

That stung, not that he was going to let her see it. What was wrong with his personality? What did that dumb little dentist have that he didn't?

'I'm not good at the people end of the business. So what? I've got more offers to build houses than I know what to do with. What changes did they want? If you promised them things I can't deliver, so help me, runt——'

'Uh-uh,' she reminded him, 'I think we made a deal.'

'It's getting to be like coming to work at a Sunday school,' he said darkly. 'All right, *Janey*, if you promised them something I can't deliver, I'll wring your scrawny little neck.'

'She wanted a bigger kitchen.'

The hammer in his hand flew about fifty feet and hit his truck.

'And a bay window in the dining-room.'

His tape measure followed the hammer.

'He thought an extra skylight in the upstairs master bath would be nice.'

His square flew down and rebounded off his truck. 'What did you tell them?' he asked darkly.

'Have you got anything left to throw?'

'You don't seem to be nailed down.'

'Let's see. I told her the kitchen would be fine once it was finished. I showed it to her on the blueprint so she could get some idea of its dimensions.'

'And?'

'She said it would be fine the way it is.'

'No! Are you kidding?'

'Absolutely not. She knew she could trust another woman on the kitchen. I told her I personally didn't much like bay windows, because of the heat loss. I mentioned she might not want cold spots in a house with so many babies.'

'And?'

'She seemed to lose interest in having a bay window.'

'You're a bloody genius. I think I'll call the United Nations office and see if they can use you. So, we got an extra skylight. I can live with that.'

'Well, actually I told him skylights have a tendency to build condensation anyway, and that I didn't think the bathroom would be a great place for one. I mentioned it would be fairly costly to put one in, as well.'

'Cancel that call to the United Nations. I feel like giving you a hug.'

'How about twelve bucks an hour, instead?' she suggested swiftly, but even as she said it she was mourning a moment of warmth that she was not going to have, a moment of strength that she would not be allowed to savour.

He threw back his head and he laughed. His teeth were strong and straight and white.

He was absolutely the most gorgeous man she had ever seen. An engaged woman had no business feeling the sharp physical awareness that she was feeling for a man other than her fiancé.

'You've got it, shrimp.'

'Blaze!'

'I only agreed to runt and pipsqueak, Bashful.'

She knew there were six more dwarfs. She started to laugh. Was there no winning with this man? A woman who knew the chances were nine out of ten that the man standing in front of her was a crook had no business feeling such a strong enjoyment of his sense of humour, such a strong appreciation for his intense interaction with life.

The laughter died abruptly. She had to win. And she had to remember what she had come here for. And she had to find something out soon, before all her conflicting emotions drove her crazy.

Drove her beyond the point of no return.

*   *   *

Blaze went into the employment office, hoping to adjust the information on his application for a wage supplement for Janey before it was processed.

He felt happy. His house was very nearly on schedule, despite the problems there had been. Janey had talked those people out of all those annoying extras that put him behind schedule. With any luck he'd be starting on framing a new house in another week.

He wondered if this strange feeling of happiness had anything to do with the way she'd looked with that baby on her hip.

He liked her. Dammit, he had done his best not to. He had done his best to get rid of her.

Maybe exactly for this reason. There was something risky about liking another person. Especially a woman, and especially a woman like that. Who was his equal. Who shared his sense of humour, and his drive, and his liking for hard work and the outdoors.

Who looked great in blue jeans and reminded him of buttercups.

'Heavy danger,' he muttered cheerfully to himself, borrowing an expression he had heard Clarence use.

Janey was making him feel things. Making all of them feel things. Work was different since she'd arrived. There was more laughter, less grousing, more sharing, less swearing.

'Mr Hamilton, I've been trying to reach you. There's still a problem on this application form.'

'No doubt,' he said wryly, but he felt unusually good-humoured about it.

Then again, he should have known by now to never trust happiness.

'The name our computer is spitting out on this social insurance number is not Janey Smith. Is it possible Smith is her maiden name?'

'No.' Janey was not the type who would be married twice before her twenty-fourth birthday. Janey was the type who would say 'I do' for life.

Even if she said it to the wrong man, he realised, and the air began to hiss out of that balloon of happiness within him.

'What name are you getting?' he asked.

'Jane Margaret Sandstone.'

That wilting balloon of happiness within him popped with such violent abruptness that for a moment he thought he would fall to his knees.

But he didn't. He straightened his shoulders and froze his face into absolute uncaring coldness.

'Is that right?' was all he said.

CHAPTER EIGHT

SANDSTONE.

Jane Margaret Sandstone.

Blaze left the employment office and went down to his truck. He climbed in, but made no attempt to go anywhere. He sat there, oblivious to the downtown bustle, feeling dazed and betrayed.

He had always known there was a reason he was attracted to women like Melanie: because they didn't hurt you. Melanie had her faults, and plenty of them, but she was exactly what she appeared to be—a beautiful woman preoccupied with herself.

But Janey. That was a different story. She had seemed gentle and sweet, full of kindness and goodwill. She had baked cookies and held babies and got Clarence a date. She had cried when she had inadvertently hurt Thomas. She had glowed with an inner loveliness that had pounded away at his defences until they had started to come down, brick by brick.

That kind of lie hurt. It cut right to the quick.

What did she want from him?

But he already knew.

Revenge.

The pieces of the puzzle began to take shape in his head. The look in her eyes those first few days when she had looked at him, full of anger and accusation. The accidents on the job. Her working late all by herself.

He smiled and could taste the bitterness of that smile. She had said it was because she liked it. And he had believed her. He'd bought her a hamburger, for Pete's sake.

He recalled that baffling feeling of *déjà vu* he had experienced when he had found out her father was sick.

Her father, Sam Sandstone.

He still felt unable to start the truck. He sat there with his head thrown back, resting on the back of the bench, his eyes locked on a little grime spot on the ceiling.

It had been so long ago. He'd been a young man, looking for his place in the world. He'd gone to university for two years, but he longed for freedom. It was nearly impossible to leash his energy. He couldn't be still for that long. He hated being inside. He was happier on the construction sites that he'd worked on every summer since he'd been about fourteen.

Didn't happiness count for something? Was he going to university so that he could find a job he hated doing for the rest of his life?

He'd taken matters into his own hands. Over the protests of a family who had never been anything but staunchly white collar, he'd left school. And he'd been elated when he'd landed the framing job with Sandstone. It was a huge project, the initial stages calling for thirty-two luxury condominiums.

But it hadn't taken Blaze long to realise that Sam Sandstone was a lot of bluff and bravado, and that his ambition far outstripped what he had the financial resources to pull off. At first Blaze had turned a blind eye to rather minor corner-cutting. Not putting the required layer of poly under the basement floors wasn't going to kill anyone, after all.

But one day he had come in and noticed that a foundation he had prepared for pouring the day before had been meddled with. Much of the rebar—the expensive steel rods that gave the cement its strength—had been removed overnight.

He had debated all day what to do about it. He wanted to just leave. To walk away from it. But he knew if he wanted to live with himself, walking away was not one of his choices.

He had gone to see Sandstone that night.

Sandstone had explained his strained financial situation to him, and Blaze had felt pity for him, but he couldn't back down. The meeting had ended badly with Sandstone bellowing at him that he would be ruined.

And he had been. His compliance had been the final straw in what turned out to be an already hopelessly strained financial situation. Sandcastle Condominiums had gone under before the roofs were on. Sam Sandstone's heart gave out under the stress.

Blaze had always felt lousy about the whole situation, and not because his final pay-cheque had bounced, either, but because he had had to make an ethical call, and he had made it. He had done the right thing and the only thing, but knowing that didn't stop him from remembering the girl who had opened the door that night.

She'd had long hair then, and when she had swung open that door it looked as if she had been laughing.

He had known, instantly and instinctively, that the girl would be part of the reason for Sam's runaway ambition. Sam was the type who would want the best for his girl. The best clothes, the best house, the lessons, and the trips that went with affluence.

For some reason, it was that girl, and not Sam, who had haunted him for a long time after the whole incident had come to a close.

He had known Sam's choices would affect his family. Would that girl pay the price for Sam's ambition? That girl who had grown into a woman?

That night he had seen her loyalty and her love for her father in her face, and felt some relief that Sam would have some help getting through whatever the future held. But now that love and loyalty had brought her to him, seeking revenge.

Just his luck. The best worker he'd ever had was out to get him.

He leaned forward and turned the key in the ignition. He was going to have to catch her at it. What a way to spend the weekend, he thought wearily, sitting in front of that house at night, waiting for her to come.

And praying she wouldn't.

'Jonathan, I'm not going to be able to have you over for movies tonight.'

Her fiancé was just finishing work for the day. He turned from the sink he was washing his hands in, dried them carefully, and removed his white jacket.

Janey felt herself looking at him critically. She was comparing him with Blaze and hating herself for it. Which was exactly why it was time to bring things to a close before they got even more out of control.

'Missed dates, cancelled dinners, blistered hands, a sun-burned nose. Janey, do you see what this job is doing to you?'

Couldn't he see how good she felt? At least physically, she felt strong and supple and healthy. Full of energy in a way she hadn't for years. She felt alive.

'I probably won't be doing this job for much longer,' she said. Why did she feel such a sensation of loss? It went deeper than having found a job that she liked to do, and knowing she had to walk away from it.

Perhaps that was the price she was paying for feeling it was up to her to seek justice. Perhaps this was the price that one paid for revenge.

'You won't be doing it much longer? Well, glory be! What has brought you to your senses?'

'We're almost done on this house,' she said evasively. 'I don't think Blaze is going to want me on another one.'

Not if my plan works out, she thought. It wasn't going to be much of a weekend, spending every night in front of that house waiting for him to come.

And praying that he wouldn't.

'Aren't you getting along with your boss?' Jonathan said this with undisguised pleasure. Or maybe that was too unkind. Maybe it was relief in his voice.

'Blaze and I have never got along particularly well,' she said.

That wasn't exactly true. There were times when they got along disturbingly well. Their entire relationship was peppered with laughter and sizzle and excitement and adventure. Even when they weren't seeing eye to eye it challenged her to be around Blaze, to match wits with him. Was it Blaze or the job that made her very skin tingle with awareness of how wonderful it was to be alive? She suspected it was Blaze.

Which was why this had to end.

'Can I trade you cars for the weekend?' she asked.

'Trade cars? You hate my car.'

'I don't hate it, exactly. I just don't know how you can drive something like that when there are homeless people in this city.'

'You're not going to raffle it to get one of them a home, are you?' he teased.

'Jonathan! What a good idea!'

'Forget it,' he said drily. 'Why exactly do you want to trade cars when you're so opposed to what mine is supposed to stand for? Are you trying to impress somebody?'

'No, I just don't want to be noticed.'

'Well, then, stick with your Bug. People notice Jaguars!'

'Not all people,' she said, and suddenly she felt oddly sad.

He held out the keys to her, she sensed with just a touch of reluctance.

'Oh, Janey,' he said reprovingly. 'Just look at your hands.'

She looked at them. She thought they looked pretty good, all things considered. A little sun-browned. A small, hardly noticeable callus on one, and a tiny nick on the other. Only one broken fingernail.

She met Jonathan's gaze. It was as if she could feel them physically drifting apart, the gap between them widening, like a ship pulling away from the dock. If one of them didn't jump over that space soon, it would be too late.

'Janey, be careful with it. It does handle a little differently from your car.'

'I'll be careful,' she said solemnly, but she wasn't talking about his car.

He frowned. 'Janey, you aren't planning something foolhardy, are you?'

'You know me better than that.'

He didn't look convinced. He didn't look as if he knew her at all.

Borrowing Melanie's car might have been a mistake, Blaze thought. No matter how he tried, he could not get comfortable in the low-slung bucket seat. But his truck parked on the street would have been a dead give-away that he was here. She would never have stopped then.

If she was even coming. This was his second night on stake-out. He was glad he had never entertained any notions about being a cop.

He poured himself another cup of coffee out of his Thermos. He glanced at the car clock. Ten minutes after three. It seemed like three hours since he'd last looked at that clock, and that time it had said three minutes after three.

He scanned the street. Four of the houses in this new subdivision were finished, so there were several cars parked in driveways and on the street, though it was basically still a pretty deserted area.

Out of intense boredom, he studied the cars parked on the street. An old Nova, in need of paint. Teenage boy, he guessed, first car. A newer model station wagon, with three children's car seats in it. He grinned, imagining a mother who hadn't had time to comb her hair, and with a frenzied look in her eye. The late model New Yorker he guessed belonged to a real-estate salesman.

And the silver Jaguar. A dope dealer or a doctor, he thought. Nobody else could afford a habit like that.

He was about to look away when he thought he caught the faintest movement from inside that parked Jag. No, he thought, a trick of the moon.

Then his eyes narrowed. *A doctor's car*. Had he really thought she was going to come careening around the corner in her little red Volkswagen?

Quietly he opened the door of Melanie's car. He reached out hastily and shut off the interior light. To avoid making noise, he did not shut the door. Stealthily, he moved towards the parked car.

The sound of a handsaw scraping jarred him and he sank back into the shadows and looked at his house. That was where the sound was coming from. He studied the car again, and was convinced he had been wrong. There was no movement from the car. The saw scraped again. So, she was already up there, was she? He began to make his stealthy way up the hill.

What on earth was he going to do with her once he got her? he asked himself.

Kill her, one voice advised him.

Kiss her, said another.

The sawing noise had stopped and now it started again.

Janey woke with a start. Where was she? Self-disgust filled her. She was in Jonathan's car, and she had fallen asleep—for the second night in a row. That was not a very good way to catch a criminal. If there was a criminal.

What had woken her? She had slid quite far down in the seat and she pulled herself up and looked out of the window, then hastily ducked back down, sliding up again until only her eyes showed.

The tears came all by themselves, and she wiped angrily at them. He was here, making his way furtively up the hill, his build, his blond hair in the moonlight making his identity unmistakable.

She waited until he had disappeared inside the structure and then carefully opened the door of the vehicle, slid out and went after him.

What on earth am I going to do when I catch him? she asked herself.

As she got closer she could hear the unmistakable sound of a handsaw. She should feel triumphant, but she didn't. She felt sad. And lonely. As lonely as she had ever felt in her whole life.

The house was spooky at night, the moonlight making twisted shadows. She crept through it, towards the noise.

She hit a squeaky board. The noise stopped abruptly. She stood still, not even breathing, but the saw did not start again. Taking a deep breath, she crept forward into a pool of unbelievable darkness deep inside the house.

She put her hands in front of her, like a blind person feeling her way. Ahead she could see it was lighter, and she moved towards the light.

'Oomph.'

She had hit something. No, someone. Someone warm and hard and big.

She let out a startled scream. Instinct turned her in her tracks. She was going to run for it.

An iron grip locked around her wrist. 'Janey?' he whispered.

'The game's up, Blaze,' she said, loudly, and with far more confidence than she felt.

'If you're here,' he mused, baffled, 'who is that?'

She squinted towards the light, and saw a form, frozen against the shadows. The form suddenly burst to life, and was running.

And so was Blaze. And so was she.

The other person leapt out of the back door and sped across the broken ground towards the road. Whoever it was was small, but fear, no doubt brought on by the size of the man hot on his heels, was making him run with incredible swiftness.

'Please don't have a gun,' Janey panted as she chased after them. Or a knife, she thought as she saw Blaze reach out with one more burst of speed, an adrenalin burst that reminded her of when they put up walls, and grab the man's collar.

They both tumbled on to the road they had reached. A struggle ensued, but it was very short, given the disparity in their sizes.

By the time Janey finally ran up, Blaze was settled on the other man's chest, and had his arms pinned under his knees. The hostile face that looked up into Blaze's looked vaguely familiar to Janey.

Blaze shifted his weight off the man, and jerked him, none too gently, to his feet.

'Janey,' he said, 'I'd like you to meet Raoul, a former employee of mine.'

Janey could smell the alcohol on him from where she stood. Then she remembered where she had seen this man before. He was the man who had been fired the day she had first arrived on Blaze's building site.

'Were you getting back at Blaze for firing you?' she asked him.

Black eyes met hers with such fury that she flinched.

'I've been fired before,' he said, his voice a drunken growl. 'But I ain't never been replaced by a woman. That made me a laughing-stock in this industry. I'm not going to be laughed at. Do you understand?'

'Sure, pal, we understand,' Blaze said patiently.

His eyes met Janey's over Raoul's head. She was surprised by the compassion she saw in those eyes that night had changed to a different shade of blue.

'Janey, why don't you go over to one of those houses and call the police?'

She nodded and went.

The police came in very short order, and took Raoul away.

'Come on,' Blaze said, 'I've got some coffee left in my Thermos. You and I need to talk.'

She didn't want to get in a car with him. She remembered, too well, how those big shoulders filled small places.

'I've got a blanket in Jonathan's car. We could go up to the house.'

Amusement tugged at the line of his mouth, as if he knew what troubled her, but for once he said nothing, just nodded.

She got the blanket and he got the Thermos and a package of those gluey cinnamon buns that graced convenience store shelves for weeks, miraculously never moulding.

They went through the house to the back veranda. She sat down, trailing her feet over the side. To her discomfort, he sat right beside her, draping the blanket casually over both their shoulders.

Dammit! Didn't he know it was his shoulders she was trying to avoid? Still, she didn't pull away. There was something oddly comforting about sitting like this with him, shoulder to shoulder, the blanket wrapped around them, sipping coffee and watching the sky get lighter.

'I felt sorry for Raoul,' she finally said.

'Yeah, me too. I talked to him after you went to the phone. I told him I thought if he got some help the judge might go easier on him. I don't know if he could hear me or not. Poor guy was pretty far gone. He used to come to work like that.'

'Sometimes you sure surprise me, Blaze Hamilton,' she admitted softly.

'I know. You want to believe I'm a really rotten guy, don't you, Janey Sandstone?'

She flinched. 'You know,' she whispered, but somehow she was disinclined to move away from the warmth of his big shoulder. 'How long have you known?'

'Since yesterday afternoon. The employment office told me. I jumped to the immediate conclusion it was you vandalising my job.'

'Don't be silly,' she said matter-of-factly. 'If I wanted to vandalise your job, I wouldn't have to work for you. I'd just sneak up here after dark, exactly like he was doing.'

'Then what do you want, Janey?' he asked softly. 'What do you want from me? Why were you here tonight?'

'I thought maybe it was you vandalising your own job. I couldn't figure out why you would do it. Insurance. Bilking the home owners.'

'You wanted it to be me, didn't you?'

'Yes,' she said. She tilted her head and looked up at his strong profile. 'Yes, I wanted it to be you.'

Her eyes clouded with tears, and she turned hastily away. 'Blaze, I saw you paying the building inspector.'

'You saw me *what*?' he bellowed.

'I saw you giving the building inspector money. Why? What are you doing?'

'I am not doing anything, you sawed-off little excuse for a human being, and I sure as hell am not paying the building inspector. What would give you such a notion?'

'How can you lie with such convincing outrage?' she asked sadly. 'I know what I saw: money. Changing palms.'

'"Money. Changing palms",' he echoed incredulously. 'You're crazy. Oh, hell, no, you're not.'

'I knew it,' she said smugly, but her smugness was tempered with sadness.

'I had a bet with him.'

'A bet? Like on a hockey game or something?' she said with disbelief.

'Yeah. Or something.'

'Sure, Blaze. I don't believe that.'

'Because you don't want to.'

'Well, what was the bet, then?'

'I had bet him that by the time he inspected my house again you wouldn't be working for me any more.' He said this with a certain self-mocking humour.

And she knew he was telling the truth. She believed him. She tried hard to look away. It felt as if her pain and her humiliation were like a raw wound on her face. But he wouldn't let her. His hand came round and gently tugged at her chin.

'Why did you want it to be me?' he asked. 'Because of this?'

She could see what was coming. If she weren't so tired, so confused, she might have been able to defend herself. But as it was she felt the oddest sensation of surrender as his lips dropped over hers.

Warm lips. Soft as a summer rain. Coffee-flavoured kisses. Light at first, like raindrops splashing down, falling on her lips and then the tip of her nose and then on her lips again, and then on her earlobes, and her neck . . . and her lips again.

The lightness disappeared, and she could sense the hunger in him. It was as if he had been hungry for her for a long time and could not get enough of her.

With gentle insistence he commanded her mouth to open beneath his. All the playfulness was gone as his tongue speared into her mouth, ravaged her, took from her, until it seemed that she had no choice left but to give . . .

Her defences, scant as they had been, scattered like dandelion fluff on the wind. She met his lips, his tongue, his mouth, his heat. She met them, embraced them, gave herself over to them.

The fire on her lips moved to her belly, as his strong hand found its way beneath her sweater to the silk of her shoulders. Her skin tingled with an awareness, and her heart sighed and accepted its homecoming.

With a boldness she had never had before, she followed his lead, and reached a tentative hand past the rich leather of his jacket, underneath the fleece of his sweatshirt. She sought the heat of his skin—the skin she had looked at so often, and yearned to touch.

She gave herself over to temptation. She felt his skin. It was smooth and resilient beneath her fingers. She allowed her hand to creep up to the hard strength of his glorious chest. She touched him and then she gave herself over to knowing his mouth, his eyes, the curve of his ear, the column of his neck.

It felt as if she had been waiting all her life for this moment. She was stunned when he put her gently away from him. She looked at him with dazed eyes, not comprehending anything except that she wanted to explore him *forever*.

'Is that why you wanted it to be me, Janey?'

She felt disorientated. What was he asking for?

'Was it the biggest betrayal of all to be wanting the man who had hurt your father so badly? But if I was dishonest, crooked, insensitive, mean, you could kill two birds with one stone, couldn't you? You thought you could kill your desire for me and have revenge both.'

She stared at him helplessly.

'And now you can't have either.'

She was still locked in his arms, his words falling on her like blows.

She pushed at him. 'Let me go.'

He did, immediately. She was not thrilled with his compliance.

'You're right,' he said softly. 'You need to sort a lot of things out before this happens.'

'*This* will never happen,' she said, leaping to her feet, and glaring at him. 'You killed my father.'

'Did he die, Janey?' He rose, the gentle concern in his face nearly breaking her heart.

'There are many kinds of death, and he died a long time ago. Eight years ago. And you did it.'

'Janey, I didn't do it. He did it himself.'

'No,' she screamed, 'he didn't. He was strong. And good. He was wonderful in every way, and you destroyed that. You destroyed a good man with your greed and ambition.'

'A good man was destroyed by greed and ambition,' he agreed. 'But it was his own, not mine.'

She hit him across the face with her open palm with all her might. The strength of her blow turned his head. She wished he'd hit back, prove once and for all that he was a complete brute, a fiend, the type who preyed on old men and women, and those weaker than him.

His hands remained at his sides. When he looked back at her there was enormous sadness in his eyes, as though he pitied her. And then she turned and ran from him, her sobs hanging in the stillness of the pre-dawn air.

He let her go. There was nothing else he could do. Except wait.

He had the oddest feeling—as though he had spent his whole life waiting for Janey. He shook it off. She had lied to him in the worst possible way. Even if it wasn't her who was trying to wreck his house, she had been trying to ruin him.

He suddenly felt exhausted.

Ever since that lemon-scented little twerp had entered his life he always seemed to feel either exhausted or exhilarated.

Consider yourself lucky, he ordered himself sternly, that you never even asked her for a date.

She'd wreaked quite enough havoc from just being in his life professionally. He should thank his lucky stars for whatever sense of self-preservation it was that had kept him from involving her in his personal life.

Melanie. He remembered the reason. He sighed. He was going to have to have a talk with Melanie.

*   *   *

Janey pulled up outside her house and got out of the car. She was so tired she was staggering. She stopped.

Her house, a little square box, in a neighbourhood of little square boxes and big trees, had a light shining out of every window.

She took a deep breath and went up her path and in the front door. One, two, three big brothers, she counted. And one Jonathan.

'What is going on here?'

'Janey!' four male voices called, and they were all around her, each of them asking questions and each raising his voice to be heard over the other, until they were all yelling.

'Shut up,' she finally exploded. She sank on to a kitchen chair. 'What is going on here?'

'Janey,' Jonathan explained, 'I was just driving by at about midnight, and I noticed you weren't home, and I remembered thinking there was something unusual about you wanting to borrow my car... and... and where the heck have you been?'

'None of your business,' she said. 'Any of you. I am a grown woman, and I cannot believe you are all behaving like this.'

'We were just worried about you, Janey,' the youngest of her brothers said. 'That's not a crime, is it? It's not like you to be out... wherever... in the middle of the night.'

She knew he would have given his eye-teeth to fill in that 'wherever' with a specific, but she was feeling rebellious and querulous.

'I went out. I could have been with a sick friend. I could have decided to have a holiday for the weekend.

I could have gone for groceries at the all-night grocery store.'

'But you weren't, were you?' said Jonathan softly. 'You were with him, weren't you?'

'Oh, Jonathan, it's a long story, and it's not what you think.'

'You were with him,' Jonathan said coldly.

'Not precisely. I mean, I didn't plan to be with him.' Her lips felt as if maybe they were blinking on and off like neon signs. *He kissed me. He kissed me. He kissed me.*

And her overtired mind added, And I liked being kissed by him better than I like being kissed by you.

She could feel the tears coming to her eyes.

'OK, guys.' Her oldest brother, Simon, took charge. 'Janey's safe. And she's tired. Let's clear out. She can fill us in on her adventure tomorrow, if she wants to.'

He said this final one with a faint look of warning, and succeeded in herding her other three protectors out of the door.

She closed her eyes, then opened them to see Simon still standing there.

'I knew it was too good to be true.'

'Janey, I want to know why you're working for Blaze Hamilton.' He sat down across the table from her.

'It's not as disloyal as you probably think,' she mumbled.

'Why would it be disloyal?' he asked sternly.

'Oh, come on, Simon. You recognised the name right away. You know who he is.'

'Yeah, about the best bloody builder in this Valley.'

'That's not what I mean.'

'What do you mean, Janey?'

'Blaze Hamilton destroyed Dad. I've never forgotten that, even if you have!'

'That's what I was afraid of,' her brother said wearily.

'What does that mean?' she asked defensively.

'Janey, you always kind of idolised Dad. Maybe that was OK for a sixteen-year-old kid, but it's time you faced the truth about the old man.'

'I don't want to hear this,' she said firmly. 'I want you to leave.'

'So you already sort of know, don't you? Deep in your heart, you know exactly what I'm going to say.'

'Stop it, Simon.'

'I don't want you trying to take on Blaze Hamilton. Especially over some misconception you've nursed inside your own mind for far too long.'

'Simon——'

'Blaze didn't make the old man go under, Janey. You were the only one who never got it.'

'I'll never speak to you again if you don't shut up.'

'He caught him. He caught the old man cutting corners and he did what he had to do. He made him bring the building up to snuff when he couldn't afford to.'

'You're lying.'

'Janey, I'm not saying Dad was a bad man. But he grew up dirt-poor and somehow he got it in his head that money was what made a man. Things. He wanted you to be able to hold your head up in a way he never could. It was his obsession. And, like a lot of obsessions, it was his Waterloo, too, Janey. It was tragic when it happened. I always felt Blaze probably felt badly about it.

'He's a good man, Janey. I think that's something else you already know in your heart of hearts, isn't it?'

'I love Jonathan.'

'That's funny. I didn't say you didn't. I always wondered something about you and Jonathan, though. I always wondered if Dad passed you a dream that you knew Jonathan could fulfil. But is it really your dream?'

'I do love him!'

Her brother sighed. 'You're tired, pet. Go to bed. Get some sleep. Things will look clearer in the morning.'

'I won't ever believe you about Dad. Not ever.'

'Won't you? Maybe you'd believe him, then. Why don't you ask Dad about Sandcastle and Blaze Hamilton?'

Her brother got up. A big man. A strong man. A man who had always seen things so clearly.

'Goodnight, Janey.' He gave her a gentle kiss on the forehead.

Somehow she knew what was left of this night was not going to be good at all.

CHAPTER NINE

JANEY fiddled with the flowers she had brought, baby's breath and daisies. She had brought flowers that reminded her of spring, even though it was autumn. Autumn was too painful—a time before the dying.

But she kept her back carefully to him, wishing the task that had brought her here would go away.

'Janey, come sit here on the edge of the bed,' he whispered. 'You look so tired. Come tell Papa what's bothering you.'

She turned and smiled. She had never been able to hide anything from him. She had not slept, and she knew the strain and fatigue were in her face.

For a moment, they studied each other. He looked no better than she, she decided, but he did not have a lack of sleep to blame it on. There was a frightening bluish-grey tinge to his skin.

And yet there was something in his eyes she was not sure she had ever seen before. Peace? Her father had never been a peaceful man. Not even before the incident with Blaze.

Even as a child, she could remember that bouncy nervous energy, and him smoking cigarette after anxious cigarette.

She went and sat on the bed, took his hand in hers. Once it had been a strong hand. Incredibly strong. Now it was weak and blue-veined.

What will Blaze's hand look like when he is old?

She tried to banish the renegade thought from her mind. She would never know. She didn't want to know.

Yes, she did.

'Dad,' she said slowly, 'could you tell me about Blaze Hamilton?'

His eyes widened briefly, and then he looked silently by her, out of the hospital window.

'You don't have to,' she said hurriedly. 'I mean if it upsets you to think about what he did to you.'

'No,' he said slowly, 'I want to tell you. I just need to collect my thoughts for a moment.' Finally, he took a deep breath. 'Janey, I maligned an innocent man to you and the time has come for me to clear my slate. I'm going to die soon, you know.'

'Dad, don't say that.'

'I almost wonder,' he said softly, 'if I wasn't waiting for this. My chance to right a wrong.

'Janey, it wasn't Blaze Hamilton's fault that the Sandcastle development went under. It was my own. I was grandiose and greedy, and I wanted so badly to be a huge success in the community. But it was too big for me, and when I started to get into trouble I cut some corners in the construction end. Blaze caught me, and made me conform to the building code—never mind the standards I had promised in my sales literature.'

'But Daddy, you kept saying it was his fault. I heard you over and over again blaming him.'

'Just to you, Janey,' he said softly, looking at her with such grave affection that it made her weep. 'Your mother and the boys knew the truth, but I was your hero. And I liked being your hero. I didn't want you to know the truth about me—that I had cheated and put people's safety at risk for my own advancement. I was the biggest failure in town, but I still wanted to be your hero. Isn't that a silly thing for a grown man to admit? I blamed Blaze so you wouldn't know how low I had sunk. I blamed Blaze so you would always look at me with those same stars in your eyes.'

She smiled at him through the tears. 'It doesn't matter. You will always be my hero.'

'You see? Those stars are still in your eyes, after all.' He closed his own eyes. 'I should have trusted love. Love forgives and accepts. Always.'

'Always,' she agreed huskily, the tears clogging her throat.

'You know, Janey, I'm glad Blaze caught me.'

'What?'

'I would have spent the last years of my life *knowing* what I had done. Maybe I could have gotten away with it. Maybe I would have been successful on the outside, but if I felt guilt and shame on the inside, what good would it have done? I'm going to my Creator with a clear conscience. When I stand at heaven's gate, I can say proudly, Sam Sandstone here.

'I kept thinking there was one more thing I had to do before I could go. Now I've done it. Thank you for asking me about Blaze.' He paused, then opened his eyes. 'Why on earth did you ask me about Blaze today?'

Haltingly she confessed her botched attempt at revenge.

Her father was laughing when she was finished. His laughter sounded so good. It was robust, the way she remembered it being long ago.

'Janey, do you see how wonderful life is? How completely full of adventure and wonder? Do you see the marvellous irony of it all? You went there to hate him, and instead——'

'Daddy?'

Something had changed in his eyes. Now she heard the change in his voice, too.

'There is only one thing in all of life that is worth pursuing with your whole heart and soul, Janey. There is only one thing worth having.'

'Daddy?'

The change was happening rapidly now. His spirit was drifting away. She could feel it, and she knew she was as powerless to stop it as she was to stop the cycles of the seasons.

'Love,' he whispered, and the most incredible smile came on to his face and his eyes shone with a light like she had never seen before.

'Love.' He spoke it as a greeting, his voice soft with reverence. 'Sam Sandstone here.'

And then the light went out. Her father was dead.

Hours later it felt as if she had made a thousand painful phone calls. Her mind was in a fog, her grief fresh and throbbing within her breast.

And yet there was one more phone call she needed to make. She told herself it was because she knew she had an apology to make. But it was more than that.

She needed him. Right now she needed as she had never needed in her entire life. She did not have the strength or the clarity to ask herself why him. She only knew it was so.

She dialled his number slowly, waiting for the sound of his voice the way a drowning person might wait for the life-jacket.

'Hello?' The voice that answered the phone was breathless, and very feminine.

'Is Blaze there?' She struggled to keep her words steady, to keep the naked need out of her voice.

'He is, but he's sleeping.' The words came out a purr of sensual satisfaction. 'Can I take a message?'

'No. Yes. Would you tell him Janey called? There's been a death in my family. I won't be able to be at work on Monday.'

He would know, she thought. He would know it was her father. He would know her need.

She had seen him, even though it was the part of himself he didn't show the world. In unexpected flashes she had seen who Blaze Hamilton really was over and over again. Under all the steel, Blaze Hamilton was gold. Pure gold. He would come to her.

She set down the phone feeling relieved. He would come to her.

'Hi, Mel.' Blaze came out of the bedroom, shirtless, and in bare feet. He stretched.

'I dislike it when you call me Mel,' she said chillily.

'Give me a break. I just woke up. When did you get here?'

'Just a few minutes ago. I knocked at the door, and when you didn't answer I let myself in. I saw my car out there, so I figured you were home.'

'Hmm.' He went to the fridge and looked inside. There was a can of open sardines in there that were beginning to look and smell fairly dangerous. He opted for the single other item in the fridge.

He popped the lid and took a deep swig of cola.

'It's not like you to be asleep during the day.' Her eyes had narrowed with a cat-like craft. 'Rough night?'

'Yeah. Found the guy who's been messing around with my house.'

'Oh.' There was relief in the way she said that.

And it was relief that he could not bring himself to harbour. She knew. She had probably known for days that he was drifting away from her. Maybe she had even known before he did. There was no sense dragging it out.

'Melanie, we need to talk.'

'Oh, dear. I don't think I like the way you said that.'

'Melanie, I like you. We've had some great times together.'

'Don't say any more. Please.'

'I'm sorry,' he said softly.

'It's her, isn't it?'

He wanted to play the innocent. He wanted to say, Who? and then act outraged when she named her suspect.

But he didn't have that kind of dishonesty within him, so he said nothing.

'I guess I had great hopes for us,' she said with brittle control.

'We don't have anything in common,' he said gently. 'We've tried to find a middle ground, but we never have.'

'I thought we were extremely compatible in some ways,' she said, and remembered passion was in her voice and her eyes.

'Melanie, I'm not a teenager any more. I want more from a relationship than that.'

'And that little thing in her carpenter's apron can give it to you? She can give you something that *I* can't?'

'I don't know. Last time I talked to her she pretty much hated my guts. She may never talk to me again. But she at least made me aware of what I should be looking for in a relationship.'

'And what is that?'

'Mel——'

'No! Tell me!'

'It's just a feeling. A warm feeling. An alive feeling. An eager feeling. All mixed in with respect and liking, and laughing at the same things.'

'Forgive me, but that sounds just a trifle dull.'

'That's what I mean about us being different, Melanie. I'm a simple man. I like blue jeans and pick-up trucks and Joe burgers. I like sunshine and sweat and the smell of sawdust.'

'I guess it's true. We are very different,' she conceded. Her eyes drifted around the room, looking for a place to settle. They settled on the paintings above his sofa. 'Those paintings I picked are an example. You never much liked them, did you?'

'They're just not my style, Melanie.'

'I guess we can't all like bullfighters on black velvet.'

He heard the hurt behind it and he let the snipe pass.

'Do you think . . . ?' Her voice drifted away.

'Sure. Take them.'

'Thank you. I hope we'll always be friends, Blaze. I truly do. If things don't work out——'

'Thanks.'

'I must go. I have about a million things to do this afternoon. Are these my keys here?'

He nodded. He took the paintings off the wall. She didn't offer to carry them. It would never even occur to her to carry them herself. Just as it would never occur to Janey not to.

He followed her silently out to her car. She wasn't going to cry. Did she know if she had been the kind of woman who could cry when she was hurt they'd have had a better chance'?

He put the paintings in her back seat. She got in, then wound the window down.

'I nearly forgot. There was a phone call a while ago.'

'I was going to ask you about that. It was the phone that woke me up.'

'It was just someone selling something. Magazine subscriptions, I think.'

'I don't have time for magazines.'

'That's what I thought. Nothing important.' She picked through her keys, searching out the ignition one. 'Well, Blaze.' Her smile was bright and beautiful. 'Will I see you around?'

'Sure.'

She left without squealing her tyres.

'Where the hell is that pipsqueak? It's nearly eight o'clock.'

He was talking to himself, which was not normal for him. But here he was a free man, and she wasn't going to show up? On the other hand, what did he think he was going to do, anyway? Run over to her and tell her he was available for dinner?

That would probably excite her wildly, considering the wallop she'd delivered to his cheek on their last encounter.

But surely by now she would have thought it through. Surely she would know the truth. How could she have worked with him all this time and not know the truth?

A good question, he thought. If she could be with him all this time and still believe those things, then dinner was a bad idea. Talking to her was a bad idea. Having her work here was a bad idea.

'Where is she?' he muttered to the sky.

'You mean Janey?' Clarence happened to be going by.

'Do we have any other members of the female persuasion on this crew that I should know about?' he snapped, his temper going steadily downhill as the clock ticked forward.

'Mabel said her dad died this weekend.' Clarence's eyes misted over. 'Poor kid.'

Blaze felt his heart stop.

She needed him.

Oh, sure he told himself, she had practically accused him of killing her father himself.

And yet he could not have stopped himself from going to her. Not if it meant her walloping him another hundred times. If that was what it took for her to get through the anger, to the grief, he would be there. And he would hold her after, for as long as she needed to be held.

He was running for his truck.

'Jonathan, thank you for being here. You've been so supportive.' Janey sucked in a deep breath. 'It makes it that much harder to tell you what I have to tell you.'

'Janey, it can wait. You're upset. You probably haven't had three hours' sleep in the past twenty-four hours.'

'Jonathan, I think you already know we can't get married, don't you?' she asked softly.

'Of course I know we would need to leave a respectable amount of time.'

'That's not what I mean,' she said gently.

'Oh.' Jonathan was silent for a time. 'It's him, isn't it, Janey?' he finally asked heavily.

Him, she thought sadly. The one who hadn't come. The one she had called for in her time of need, and he hadn't come.

Women were cursed with this silly, romantic self that could make any self-centred male over into what they wanted him to be. What a fool she had been to imagine a sensitive side to him. He had worked with a man who had a severe handicap for three years without noticing. He had called Clarence a demeaning nickname for even longer than that. He swore and he threw things. He had a primitive view of women.

'No,' she said firmly. 'It's not him, Jonathan, it's us. We're too different. We want very different things from life.'

'What do you mean different things?'

'I want love,' she said, remembering her father. 'You want prestige and money, and all the good times that those things buy.'

She looked at him sadly, seeing what her brother had tried to make her see—that she had tried to realise her father's failed and tragic dream through a man who had the same dream, and far more chance of attaining it.

'I'm not that superficial,' he said stiffly.

'Jonathan, please believe me that I wasn't judging you. I was just saying we're different and our differences have become so apparent over the last few weeks.'

'Since him,' Jonathan said emphatically.

'I probably won't ever see him again,' she said softly, and tears misted her eyes. She didn't bother to wipe them away. What were a few more tears? What was a little more grief in this vast ocean of grief within her?

'Janey, this is really the wrong time for you to be making a decision. Wait a few weeks. A month.'

'No.' This would be the last gift she could ever give her father—to be true to her heart.

'I'd like to be your friend anyway. Especially through this. If you need anything, and I mean anything, call me. I'll be there for you.'

'Thank you.' She closed her eyes. 'I'm so tired. I need a shower. And then I need to go to bed for a while.'

'You go have a shower. I'll look after all these flowers and then let myself out.'

'Thank you again. You've always been such a gentleman.' She kissed him gently on the cheek then padded off to the bathroom.

Blaze pulled up in front of her house. A Janey house, he decided. At first it looked plain, like a little box, and then he noticed the trees around it, and the late autumn flowers in the flowerbeds, and the cheerful yellow curtains at the kitchen window. Her plain little house glowed with an inner beauty just as she did.

He went up the stairs two at a time, but he didn't even have a chance to knock.

Her fiancé, the dentist, came out, and pulled the door firmly shut behind him.

'Blake, isn't it?' he said coolly.

Blaze saw no reason to correct him. The tiny landing seemed too small for both of them.

'I just heard about Janey's dad. I wanted to talk to her.'

'Well, she doesn't want to talk to you,' he said crisply, 'and I think, given the enormous stress she is under, it would be best to respect her wishes, don't you?'

Blaze didn't like the way he said that, as if he were talking to some insensitive oaf who would just push his way in where he wasn't wanted.

Which was probably exactly what he would do, if he wasn't being regarded with such cold disdain by Janey's man.

Janey's man. A shaft of sadness rippled through Blaze. That was why he was here, when he looked at it honestly—out of some misguided sense that *he* was Janey's man.

But he wasn't. He wasn't the one with the right to hold her, to comfort her, to say soft words to her. It wasn't his ring on her finger, or his name that came to her lips when the world seemed to be caving in all around her.

He blinked hard as that reality hit him.

'Would you tell her I came by to offer my condolences?' he said gruffly, through the lump in his throat. 'Would you tell her that?'

Had he looked again at Jonathan Peters he would have known those were words Janey was never going to hear, but he didn't. He turned and walked quickly away, and he didn't look back at the person he felt was the luckiest man in the whole world.

'Janey, I think you need to go back to work.'

'I'm not ready to look for a job yet.' She turned her

back on Mabel, concentrating ferociously on pouring boiling water into her teapot.

'Don't you have a job?' Mabel had the most beautiful voice. It was like a bird singing. It was completely out of keeping with her appearance.

Mabel was six feet three inches tall, big-boned and rangy. She had a face that was strong and kind and homely. It always reminded Janey of the Statue of Liberty.

'No, I don't have a job.'

'Well, that's not the way Clarence tells it. He says Blaze would have you back in a minute.'

Janey set down her teapot in front of her old friend. She didn't look at her, but carefully rearranged cookies on a plate.

'The last time I saw Blaze I hit him across the face as hard as I could. I haven't apologised, and I don't plan to. Does that sound like a candidate for employee of the year?'

'It sounds like a woman on an absolute emotional roller-coaster,' Mabel said placidly. 'Why not apologise?'

Janey's eyes filmed over. 'He never even offered me sympathy about my dad. I know it wasn't his fault, I know he had nothing to do with it, but he must have known what that man meant to me.'

'Oh, Janey, you know men. They just never know what to say in situations like that.'

'Clarence knew what to say,' she said with a sniff.

Mabel smiled a soft and secret smile that made her look almost pretty. 'Clarence is a very special man. But I think Blaze is, too.'

'You do? How would you know?'

'Clarence and I had dinner with him the other night. We had a special favour to ask of him.'

'And you like him?'

'Enormously. Aside from the fact he's gorgeous, he just seems so down-to-earth and real. He looked very tired, though, and sad. Something like you're looking now.'

'Blaze did?' she asked. Too late she tried to bite back her concern.

'Janey,' her friend asked gently, 'are you in love with him?'

She looked at the cookies. She looked out of the window. She ran a finger down the teapot. She said no at least a dozen times in her head, but when she opened her mouth a plaintive and lost, 'Yes,' emerged.

'Well, what are you going to do about it?'

'Nothing. Try and salvage my pride.'

'But why?'

'Because he has a woman in his life. Because he doesn't feel the same way about me. Because he couldn't even tell me he was sorry about my dad. Because I hit him and accused him of something that wasn't true, and I feel like an idiot.'

'So pride comes before love on your list, does it?'

The words stung. It was a betrayal of that final message her father had given her over a month ago.

'Mabel, I just don't know what to do. I don't know what I feel. I don't know anything. I'm scared and confused and lost.'

'For heaven's sake, then, put yourself out of your misery.'

'How?'

'Tell him.'

'I can't,' she whispered.

'Why?'

'Why would he love me? I'm plain. I'm built like a boy. I'm argumentative. I like doing men's work better than women's work.'

'Janey, you aren't plain,' her friend said tolerantly. 'I'm plain. But that is really beside the point. Maybe he'd love you because you're good and gentle and loving and sweet. Maybe he'd love you because you're independent and funny, and fierce when you need to be. Maybe he'd love you because you're spirited, and wholesome, and smart, and about a million other wonderful things.'

'Mabel, you are such a dear. But I can't just go throw myself at his size twelve boots. I'm fragile right now.'

Mabel sighed and popped an entire cookie in her mouth. She chewed with thoughtful ecstasy. 'You're making me feel guilty about being so happy.'

'Well, you can't hide it, anyway. Mabel, you're just shining. Your eyes are shining, your skin is shining, your smile could practically blind me.'

'It's Clarence. I don't know how to thank you for that man. He is every single thing I had given up hoping for. That's mostly the reason I dropped by today. To thank you, and to ask you a special favour.'

'Anything,' Janey said warmly.

'Clarence and I are going to get married in December.'

'Mabel! That's so soon!'

'I know.'

'But are you sure?'

'Positive.'

Several months ago she would have questioned someone being so positive about what they were feeling, so sure of love.

But then love made itself known. It wasn't in the least obscure. She felt deep admiration for Clarence and Mabel for saying a simple yes to all the joy love was offering them.

'I want you to stand up with me.'

'Me?'

'You introduced us. You have always been a wonderful friend to me, and now you are a wonderful friend to Clarence as well. Neither of us would hear of anyone else. Will you, Janey? Please say yes.'

'All right,' she said slowly. 'Yes.'

So, there would be a wedding in December, after all. And Blaze had been wrong. Dead wrong. The only reason people got married in December was not for a tax break.

Blaze. Suddenly a giant hand of fear squeezed at her heart.

'We had a special favour to ask of him.'

'Is Blaze going to be there?' she whispered.

'Of course,' Mabel said innocently. 'He's going to be Clarence's best man. Who else would he ask? Without Blaze guiding him he'd probably end up in a pink suit with purple polka dots on it!'

'I'm not ready to face Blaze.'

'The wedding is still a month away. You'll be ready by then, won't you?'

'No!'

'If you're still feeling as strongly about Blaze in a month then you'd better be prepared to do something about it. You'll drive yourself crazy otherwise. Maybe you'll see him and feel nothing. Wouldn't that be a relief?'

Fat chance. 'I suppose you're right,' she said dismally.

She felt as if she would go there and look pathetic. She was the one who was supposed to have got married in December. And there she'd be, no fiancé, no job, her heartbreak written all over her face.

Not that Blaze Hamilton would be sensitive enough to see it.

Jonathan had told her he would do anything for her. And he had. She wondered if his offer would stretch to include escorting her to a wedding. And not mentioning to certain people—a certain person—that their engagement had not worked out.

She sighed. She was damned poor at duplicity. She should know that by now.

But it was still worth a shot.

CHAPTER TEN

JANEY walked demurely through the double doors and down the aisle, clutching a little spray of posies, and praying she wouldn't trip over the unaccustomed length of the pale yellow gown that swirled around her feet.

And then she almost did trip. Her eyes caught on him.

He was waiting, his hands folded calmly in front of him, his big shoulders encased in the stiff formality of a black dinner-jacket. The dark black of the fabric made him look blonder than ever. For some reason he looked stronger than ever.

Her eyes moved slowly up the length of him, savouring him, appreciating him. Who would have thought Blaze Hamilton would look so fine in tails?

It had been two long months. She hoped she had imagined the pull he had on her.

But she had not. Her eyes locked on his, and the strangest feeling filled her soul. For a moment she imagined tender welcome in the blue of those eyes. For a moment she imagined it was she walking towards him, ready to give him her pledge... her promise of forever.

Someone blew his nose, and it brought her drifting mind up sharply to reality. She looked away from him, but not quickly enough. Before she looked away she saw his lip twist faintly upwards at one corner.

The look of a man who had glimpsed her soul, who had had a peek into her very private self.

And it would be the last one, she vowed. She made herself focus on Clarence.

His muddy eyes were locked on Mabel. He looked like Paul Bunyan in a white tux and tails. And he looked like a man deliciously and endlessly in love.

Janey stood aside, and with a soft rustle of yards of endless silk Mabel moved by her and took her place beside her groom. The man she would marry. The man she would hold all the days of her life. The man she would give children to.

'Dearly beloved...'

Janey sniffled loudly. She was aware that Blaze had stepped back from the nuptial couple, just as she had, and that his eyes were fastened with unrelenting interest on her face. She nosed her chin up towards the ceiling. She struggled to remain impassive, but the struggle failed miserably. The beautiful words were washing over her, making her ache with a yearning that hurt. The tears slithered down her proud face.

Clarence and Mabel exchanged their vows. Love transformed them into the most beautiful couple in the world as they softly made their promises, one to the other. Janey was trying miserably to stifle her sobs.

The minister pronounced them man and wife, and Janey quickly found her lace-edged hanky and did her best to repair her damaged face before turning to face Blaze.

She tried out her most brilliant smile. It wobbled. He rested one hand on his hip, an inviting loop for her to slide her arm through.

She would rather have died. He moved towards her, took her reluctant hand and tucked it comfortably through his arm. She hoped he could not feel her trembling. Her senses were threatening to overwhelm her. The smell of him. The feel of him. She felt as if she was quivering like a puppy too long left alone.

He patted her arm with annoying reassurance. 'I could swear you cried through the whole ceremony,' he said under his breath. 'Do you find weddings emotional, Janey? Especially since your own has been cancelled?'

'I see you are still pursuing sensitivity training with all your heart and soul,' she said just as quietly out of the side of her mouth. 'As a matter of fact, I don't find weddings the least perturbing.'

'Right. Stocks in the Kleenex corporation just leapt through the ceiling because of your stalwart lack of emotion.'

'Maybe it's that time of month,' she retorted, looking straight ahead.

He snorted back the laughter. 'Your feminist sisters would burn you at stake for that one, Ms Sandstone.'

'Sign the register, Mr Hamilton.'

'Yes, ma'am.'

He managed to behave himself as they trailed the ecstatic Clarence and Mabel out of the church.

They passed Jonathan, and Janey gave him a tiny wave. She could feel Blaze stiffen beside her.

'What's he doing here?'

'He's my escort.'

'What? Clarence told me your engagement had been called off.' Blaze snapped his mouth shut as though he regretted admitting he had shown any interest in information passed to him by Clarence.

They came out of the church. Melanie was just getting out of her sports car.

'Late as always,' Blaze murmured.

Janey felt herself stiffen at the wry affection in his voice. Melanie looked simply stunning in a tight shining pink flapper-style dress, the bottom generously embroidered with sequins. She waved at Blaze and snapped a few pictures.

'You look utterly gorgeous, darling,' she said, coming up to him as people began to come out of the church and mill about the snow-covered yard. 'I always knew you had this potential.'

'Have you met Janey Sandstone?'

'I don't believe I've had the pleasure,' Melanie said with so much syrup in her voice it was obvious she was doing her best to hide a severe lack of pleasure.

'We spoke on the phone once,' Janey reminded her. She extended her hand. 'Good to meet you.'

'You spoke on the phone once?' Blaze said thoughtfully. 'When was that?'

'Oh, ages ago,' Melanie said briefly. 'My, who is that?' Her exotic cat-like eyes had just narrowed with the look of a cougar on the hunt.

And her prey looked to be Jonathan! He did look extraordinarily dashing today. Jonathan always knew exactly what to wear to things like this.

'Janey's fiancé,' Blaze said.

'Friend,' Janey corrected.

Jonathan came up and planted a rather platonic kiss on the tip of Janey's nose. 'I suppose you'll have to do all those wedding things. Go for pictures and——' He stopped dead as his eyes fell on Melanie. 'And whatever else the wedding party does while the invited guests starve to death waiting for them to arrive at the reception,' he finished weakly.

'Jonathan, this is Blaze's——' Janey looked helplessly at Blaze.

'Friend,' he filled in helpfully.

'Melanie,' she completed the introduction, 'Jonathan Peters.'

'Dr Jonathan Peters,' Blaze said smoothly. 'Why don't you and Dr Peters keep each other company while Janey and I do all those things the wedding party does?'

'Delighted,' Jonathan said with enthusiasm.

'A doctor?' Melanie cooed, and lost no time in looping her arms through Jonathan's and moving off with him.

Blaze shot Janey an amused look. 'That man is never going to marry you,' he announced to her, opening the back door of the wedding car for Clarence and Mabel. He opened her door for her, and grinned as she slid in.

'Good thing it's not raining,' he commented. 'You'd like to drowned with your nose that high in the air.'

'Quit tormenting me about my broken engagement,' she spat at him. 'I happen to be very sensitive about it.'

'Especially at this time of the month?' he shot back irreverently.

'You two, stop it,' Mabel ordered cheerfully. 'You'll ruin the wedding pictures glowering at each other like that.'

'Janey is glowering,' Blaze said, turning and giving Mabel his most winning smile. 'I am my normal handsome self.'

Mabel laughed at the man as if he was actually funny, Janey fumed. She didn't suppose it was permissible to tell the bride not to encourage juvenile behaviour from the best man.

The best man for me, a little voice inside her whimpered traitorously.

Somehow she managed to smile for Mabel's precious pictures. The ceaseless activity was giving her a headache. Her constant vigilance in his presence not to let him see her complete and humiliating vulnerability to him was giving her a stomach ache.

As soon as the group shots were over, she fled outside to a little walled garden the photographer must have used in the summertime.

Her escape was short.

'Would you leave me alone?' she snapped.

'Why?'

'Because you have all the sensitivity of a brontosaurus in rut.'

'A subject you're familiar with?' he asked with mock-surprise.

'Blaze, you are making me crazy!'

'Am I?' he said with even more mock-surprise. 'Why do you suppose that is, Janey-is-a-buttercup?'

She closed her eyes. Sometimes in her dreams she saw them on a blanket in the middle of a verdant green pasture spotted yellow with buttercups. In the dream he touched her hair and called her that, with such grave tenderness . . .

'Did he ever make you crazy?' he asked softly. 'Did he ever haunt your every waking thought, or turn you to butter with a look, or drive you to the part of passion that is as close to the edge of sanity as we ever come?'

'My feelings for Jonathan are off limits. My engagement is off limits,' she said unsteadily. 'And for your information it was called off because of my father's death.'

It was a desperate ploy to keep him from invading her heart.

His whole tone changed. 'Janey, I was so sorry about that. I haven't had a chance to tell you that personally.'

His voice was so exactly the voice she had needed to hear that night she had called him that she turned swiftly away from him.

'Impersonally might have helped,' she muttered.

'Pardon?'

'Never mind.'

'Can I hold you?' he asked softly. He was right behind her, far too close.

'No. It's too late. I needed you then, not now!'

'You needed me then?' he repeated.

'Why do you think I called? Just to tell you I wouldn't be at work?' She hated herself for what she was giving away, for what she was letting him know—that precious secret she had guarded inside herself, a secret that felt as if she lived for it, and could be destroyed by it, too. She felt so confused.

She always felt confused around Blaze Hamilton. She turned and looked at him. 'I know I shouldn't have called, anyway. It's wrong, isn't it? To need a man who is taken?'

'Taken?'

'Taken,' she repeated. He only looked puzzled. 'By your gorgeous girlfriend.'

'Melanie isn't my girlfriend any more.'

Janey's eyes widened. 'She isn't?'

He shook his head. 'When did you call me, Janey?'

Her fists clenched at her sides. 'I called you when my dad died. I thought you'd understand. What did you want me to do? Beg you?'

'You called me, but what? I wasn't home? The phone was busy? What?'

'Melanie answered. She said she would give you the message.'

A strange look came on to his face. Rage. Pain. 'She didn't, Janey. You have to believe that.'

'Even so, what did you need? An engraved invitation? Clarence must have told you what had happened.'

A dangerous light was beginning to burn in Blaze's face. In a less civilised time a light like that might have meant a savage justice was about to be done.

'Clarence did tell me,' he told her softly. 'I went to your place right away. I did know, Janey. I knew you needed me.'

'You did?' she whispered. 'And you came even though you were Melanie's man then?'

'I was never Melanie's man. We said goodbye the day after you and I caught Raoul up at the house.'

'That's the day my dad died,' she said softly.

'Ah. Things are beginning to make sense. On Monday Clarence told me why you weren't at work. I went over to your house right away. Unfortunately, Jonathan was guarding your door, and I listened to his words instead of my own heart.' The look on his face did not bode well for Jonathan.

'You came?' she repeated.

'I came.'

'OK, you two,' Clarence bellowed out the door. 'On to the reception.'

Blaze gave her a pained look. She smiled weakly back at him.

'Have you two stopped fighting?' Mabel asked, settling herself on her cushion of silk, and looking at them keenly.

Neither of them answered.

'Ahh,' Mabel said. She cuddled close to her husband, looking like a cat who had swallowed a canary.

The guests were starving, just as Jonathan had predicted they would be, and dinner was served as soon as the bride and groom were settled. Janey sat on the right-hand side of Mabel, two whole people removed from Blaze Hamilton. Thank the lord. Maybe she could collect her scattered thoughts.

She looked out at the crowded hall. Melanie and Jonathan sat together, his head bent attentively as she shared something with him. Melanie's cheeks were glowing prettily. Jonathan's eyes were glowing lustily.

They had barely begun the sumptuous meal when they were interrupted by the tinkling of two hundred silver spoons tapping the edges of wine glasses.

Giggling, Mabel rose, and so did Clarence. To a roar of approval, they exchanged the kiss that the tradition called for. They had not been seated again for five minutes when the demand of the tinkling wine glasses went up again.

'Your turn this time,' Mabel informed her happily.

'Pardon?' Janey froze to her seat.

'You. And Blaze. It goes down the table.'

'I'm going under the table,' Janey muttered, searching frantically for a place to escape.

The call of the wine glasses was getting louder. She felt his hand on her shoulder. She glanced up at him, her eyes full of pleading. She thought his gaze would be full of that familiar amusement. But she was stunned by the hunger in his eyes, the dark passion that had turned them to sapphire.

Slowly, she scraped back her chair and rose. He took her chin in his hand, and looked down at her, his eyes drinking in her face as the tinkling threatened to shatter glasses if they didn't do something soon.

He kissed her. And he kissed her. And he kissed her. The cheer had died and little 'ooohhs' of recognition were rising from the crowd.

She was too mixed up to fight him. She gave herself into his care. She let him guide her to a place she had never been before.

In front of *two hundred* people, the voice of sanity finally interrupted. She pulled away from him. He was smiling a smile so lazy and sensuous that it did nothing to put out the fire within her.

His lazy eyes drifted outwards and, startled, she followed his glance.

He was looking at Melanie and Jonathan.

Her heart sank. Had it only been pay-back time that had motivated the length and passion of that kiss?

Jonathan and Melanie were so deep in conversation that they seemed to have failed to notice the kiss.

Blaze actually laughed. He looked at her. 'Life has its own rewards and punishments, doesn't it? There are two people who absolutely deserve each other.'

She discovered that her knees felt wobbly. She hastily sat down to her dinner.

After dinner, there were speeches and toasts, and more speeches, and finally the tables were broken up to make room for the first dance.

Janey stood there, feeling self-conscious and overwhelmed. Blaze came and stood beside her. 'Did I tell you how lovely you look?'

'No, but thank you.'

'I like you better in blue jeans.'

I like you better in blue jeans, too. 'I think we've done our loyal duty,' she said nervously. 'I think we can just split up now and go our separate ways.' He didn't move. 'Can't we?'

'I think we participate in this first dance.'

'Oh.'

The lights went down and hopelessly romantic music filled the room. Clarence held out his arms to Mabel. They were two big people. Clumsy, even, in normal circumstances. But tonight they were a prince and a princess, made graceful by the connection in their eyes, in the way they held each other. The room might have been empty, save for them, looking at one another.

Joyful tears ran unchecked down Clarence's face.

She saw Blaze take a suspicious swipe across his own eyes. But when he turned to her his eyes seemed as clear as ever, as unreadable as ever.

'Our turn,' he said, holding out his arm to her.

She hesitated. And then she knew exactly how Clarence and Mabel had felt. It was as if the room grew small and dark and empty. There was only him, and her, his eyes guiding her through some night that she had travelled alone for too long, his arms warming her against a cold she had not known existed right in the centre of a heart that suddenly felt full.

'Marry me,' he whispered.

'What?' She stopped. People turned and looked at her. She quieted her voice. 'Don't be absurd.'

Her heart was beating a million miles a minute. Was this another of his jokes? Another of his insensitivities? Was he riding the tide of romantic energy weddings created, being impulsive, saying something he would regret the instant he saw she took him seriously?

She wanted to believe him. But she felt it would kill her if he was kidding.

She turned and searched the room. 'Where is Jonathan? I should at least check in with him. He is my date.'

Blaze looked mildly annoyed, but smiled with a certain predatory patience that unnerved her.

'Why not marry me?' he said, as he followed her to where Jonathan and Melanie sat.

'We barely know each other,' she whispered fiercely at him. She smiled at Melanie. 'I don't even know your real name,' she said to him in an undertone.

'We were just discussing dream holidays,' Melanie said brightly. 'Listen to this.'

Janey listened with her ears, but her heart was a million miles away. She looked nervously at Blaze, who was rolling his eyes as Melanie chattered about the Riviera, and Paris and flowers and strolls and gourmet meals.

'Personally,' Blaze said, 'my idea of a holiday is a rifle, a horse, a campfire and a someone to share the stars with.'

Jonathan's smile left no room to doubt that he felt a cretin had arrived at their table.

'How about you, Janey?' Blaze asked softly. 'Paris, or a one-man sleeping-bag with two people in it?'

'I don't know,' she said sharply.

'That's no way to get to know each other,' he reprimanded her lightly.

'Oh, Janey loves tents and campfires and all that stuff,' Jonathan said indulgently. 'Remember you tried to talk me into a three-day hike, once.' He turned to Melanie. '*Three days.*' As if that were the equivalent of asking him to spend three days staked out to an ant hill with a mess of honey on his belly.

'*Three days*?' Melanie said with a shriek of laughter. 'Without a shower?'

Blaze was smiling at her, Janey, that slow lazy smile that made her so nervous.

'Blair,' he informed her in a low tone, 'and don't tell me I don't know you.'

'Well, you don't.' She got up from the table, and looked around frantically for an exit. She saw some doors that headed out on to a patio, and charged towards them.

She paused for a long time outside, breathing in the silence, the cool December air.

'Marry me.'

She nearly jumped out of her skin.

'Are you drunk?'

'I don't drink. You might want to mark that on the pro side of your future-mate checklist.'

'I've asked you to leave me alone.'

'You can put that on the con side. Persistent. Doesn't give up until he gets what he wants.'

She tried to change the subject. 'You don't prefer to be called Blair, do you?'

'God, no. Blair goes on the con side.'

'There is no pro side or con side. I don't have a future-mate checklist. You're not being rational. You know that, don't you?'

'Yeah, I know. I haven't had a rational thought since September. Since a certain day in September when a little buttercup showed up on my job site and started throwing her weight around. All ninety-nine pounds of it.'

'It was wrong of me to go to work for you,' she said in a tiny voice.

'That's a girl. Spit it out so we can get on with our lives.'

'I only wanted to work for you because I thought you were a crook. I thought you had blackmailed my father. I thought you had done something despicable and cold and callous and cruel that had destroyed him, the man I loved most in the world.'

'And?'

'And I found out you weren't any of the things I wanted you to be.'

'Your father told you that?'

'He did. But a long time after I had already discovered it for myself.'

'Janey, you must know something about a man you wanted to hate and couldn't.'

She ignored that. 'Anyway, I've owed you an apology for some time, and now I've made it. And I'm sorry I hit you that night, as well. That was unforgivable.'

'I love it when you do that,' he said softly.

'What?' she asked suspiciously.

'Point your little chin at the sky, and fold your hands carefully in front of you just like a proper Victorian miss.'

'Are you making fun of me?'

'No. I accept your apology.'

'Thank you,' she said primly.

'I bet I could coax the wildcat out in you,' he said with soft challenge.

She almost leapt back from him. 'Don't you dare, Blaze Hamilton.'

'I suppose you want to wait until after we're married,' he said with disgust.

'We are not getting married.'

'Why not?'

'I told you. We barely know each other.'

'OK, tell me everything you think I should know about you. That should take about fifteen minutes.'

'I happen to be more complicated than that,' she said indignantly.

'The complicated part,' he said softly, 'I already know all about. The complicated part is the part that haunts me, and makes me wake up with your name on my lips. The complicated part is how a man reacts to a certain perfume, to a certain voice, to a certain quirk of a certain pair of lips. The complicated part is feeling alive and full of wonder at the hands of a woman you never even would have asked for a date. The complicated part is starting to believe in things you thought you'd outgrown, things you'd relegated to romantic hogwash a long time ago.

'There. That's the complicated part. You have fifteen minutes to tell me the rest of it. Your favourite colour, and the flowers you like best, and where you went to school, and what kind of dog you want to have.

'But don't try and tell me about the complicated part.'

'Blaze,' she whispered, her eyes wide with wonder. 'What are you saying?'

'Come on, Janey. You're the most intelligent woman I ever met. I don't have to spell it out for you.'

'Yes, you do.'

'Hell, Janey you're going to make me say it, aren't you?'

'Yes,' she whispered.

He smiled. That same smile she thought she had seen when she came down that aisle. A smile of unbelievable tenderness, of welcome.

'I love you,' he said gravely.

She blinked back the tears. She opened her mouth but no words would come past the lump in her throat.

He scowled at her. 'I suppose that isn't good enough? I have to say it all? OK, shrimp, I love you beyond reason. I love you even though I have tried not to. I can't get the taste of your mouth out of my mind. I think tormented thoughts about how you fill out your blue jeans. I hate going to work in the morning when you aren't going to be there——'

'Blaze——'

'No, you asked for it. Don't interrupt me now. Babies make me feel all soft inside. I damn near started bawling at the way Clarence and Mabel looked at each other tonight, because I want us to be looking at each other like that——'

'Blaze——'

'A few months ago I wouldn't have even hesitated to punch Jonathan in the face as hard as I could for lying to me the way he did. For daring to put himself in my way. But I'm quieter inside. I'm different. Loving you is making me different. Happier. More interested in other people. More able to see them. Less of a human bulldozer——'

'Blaze——'

'I have always dreamed of marrying a woman who could bake cookies.'

'Blaze——'

'No. One more thing. I've always chosen to be involved with women who couldn't make me feel this way. Because, dammit, Janey, this is the hardest, scariest thing I've ever done, standing here before you with my heart in my hands, hoping and praying that somewhere, somehow, I've done something to make me worthy of your love. Worthy of you feeling in return all the things I'm feeling.'

'I do,' she whispered. 'I feel all those things. Every single one.'

'You do?'

She nodded. 'I do.'

'Do you enough to say "I do"?'

She laughed. 'Yes. That much.'

'Soon? Next week?'

'The only reason people get married in December, Blaze, is for a tax break,' she informed him demurely.

'Who fed you that line?'

'You did.'

'I was wrong. Put it on the con side. Occasionally he's wrong.' He sobered. 'If you wanted to wait, though, out of respect to your father's memory, I will try to understand that.'

'Thank you, Blaze,' she said softly. 'It means a lot to me that you would offer that in memory of a man I know you didn't have much reason to respect.'

'Oh, Janey, I never thought your dad was a bad man, just a human one, facing life's temptations and challenges the way we all do as we struggle to find our way home.'

'I don't think we need to wait,' she said. 'The most respectful thing I could do for my father's memory is pursue the one thing worth having with my whole heart and soul.'

'Love?'

'Yes, love. I started building a house with you, and instead I found my way home.'

'My little homemaker. I've missed you so much,' he said, holding her tight.

'Blaze,' she murmured contentedly, 'could we see about that wildcat now?'

'Sure we can, Janey-is-a-wildcat.'

ANNOUNCING THE

PRIZE SURPRISE SWEEPSTAKES!

This month's prize:

L-A-R-G-E—SCREEN PANASONIC TV!

This month, as a special surprise, we're giving away a fabulous FREE TV!

Imagine how delighted you and your family will be to own this brand-new 31" Panasonic** television! It comes with all the latest high-tech features, like a SuperFlat picture tube for a clear, crisp picture...unified remote control...closed-caption decoder...clock and sleep timer, and much more!

The facing page contains two Entry Coupons (as does every book you received this shipment). Complete and return *all* the entry coupons; **the more times you enter, the better your chances of winning the TV!**

Then keep your fingers crossed, because you'll find out by July 15, 1995 if you're the winner!

Remember: The more times you enter, the better your chances of winning!*

*NO PURCHASE OR OBLIGATION TO CONTINUE BEING A SUBSCRIBER NECESSARY TO ENTER. SEE THE REVERSE SIDE OF ANY ENTRY COUPON FOR ALTERNATE MEANS OF ENTRY.

**THE PROPRIETORS OF THE TRADEMARK ARE NOT ASSOCIATED WITH THIS PROMOTION.

PTV KAL